BALZAC

Gillette
or
The Unknown Masterpiece

The Menard Press
London
1988

Cover design by Julia Farrer

UK representation by Password
25 Horsell Road, London N5 1XL.
Tel. 01–607 1154

US & Canadian distribution:
SPD Inc., 1814 San Pablo Avenue, Berkeley, Cal. 94702, USA.

ISBN 0 903400 99 5

The Menard Press
8 The Oaks
Woodside Avenue
London N12 8AR
Tel. 01–446 5571

Typeset by Fakenham Photosetting Ltd
Printed by Camelot Press PLC

To Audrey

....
....
....
....
....
....

1988

Denn das ist Schuld, wenn irgendeines Schuld ist:
die Freiheit eines Lieben nicht vermehren
um alle Freiheit, die man in sich aufbringt.
Wir haben, wo wir lieben, ja nur dies:
einander lassen; denn dass wir uns halten,
das fällt uns leicht und ist nicht erst zu lernen.

(Rilke)

PREFACE AND ACKNOWLEDGMENTS

When I first became possessed by this story several years ago I knew nothing about the literature on it – which was not altogether my fault since much of it was still being written. Not until I began drafting the translation in 1987 and researching the story's background did I, to my amazement, discover whole books about *Gillette*, written during the time of my own involvement. The essay (as well as the translation) could not have been attempted without plundering this literature. To have footnoted everything would have been clumsy, even if feasible, but all sources are listed whether or not my thefts are acknowledged in the text. I am grateful to the writers for forcing me to generate some new thoughts about the story while I engaged in that most intense version of reading, which is translation. I hope these thoughts will add a modest footnote to the growing (and growing) literature surrounding Balzac's no longer unknown masterpiece. But the primary offering, and the reason for this book's being, is the translation.

An early draft of the translation was read by my old friends and fellow travellers in French literature, Jonathan Griffin and Peter Hoy. Their comments were, as usual, perceptive, uninhibited and informed by the best interests of the text. I am grateful to Peter Hoy for organising hospitality in Oxford at his college, Merton, for arranging library facilities at the Taylorian and for expert advice on bibliographical style. Stephen Bann, Keith Bosley, Vanessa Davies, Richard Freeborn, Victor Osborne and Stuart Brenton made helpful suggestions about specific problems.

Dr Vanessa Davies made invaluable detailed comments on a draft of the essay as well as insisting, quite rightly, that I reorganise it. Helpful thoughts came from Keith Bosley (continuing our twenty year conversation about works in progress), my ex-cousin-in-law Diana Douglas, Musa (the Turk) Farhi, and Barbara Rosenbaum. I am grateful to three painters, Julia Farrer, Audrey Jones and Willow Winston, for patiently contributing to my (visual) education. Thanks too to the painter Josef Herman – it is good to be in renewed dialogue with him after several years, and a bonus to discover he has always loved the Balzac story. Thanks, finally, to Yves Bonnefoy for his words in the Ashmolean, between the Poussin and the Uccello, about the heart and mind of the *Belle Noiseuse*.

4

CONTENTS

Note

1. It is advisable to read the story before the essay, though the Dramatis Personae section can be consulted.

2. All passages in the essay in single quotation marks are from the story. All passages in double quotation marks are from other texts or there for some other reason.

GILLETTE
or
THE UNKNOWN MASTERPIECE

To a Lord

....
....
....
....

1845

I

GILLETTE

It was a cold December morning; 1612 was drawing to an end. A young man whose clothing looked threadbare was walking up and down before the gate of a house in the rue des Grands-Augustins in Paris. After to-ing and fro-ing for quite some time with the lack of resolve of a lover not daring to enter the presence of his first mistress, however welcoming she might be, he finally crossed the threshold and asked at the gate if Master François Porbus was at home. Receiving the answer yes from an old woman engaged in sweeping out a low-ceilinged room, the young man slowly climbed the stairs – stopping now and then like a newly-arrived courtier anxious about his reception by the King. When he arrived at the top of the spiral staircase, he stood still for a moment on the landing, unsure whether to lift the grotesque knocker resplendent on the door of the studio where the man who painted Henri IV was doubt-less hard at work – the man the queen mother, Marie de Medici, later forsook for Rubens. The young man felt that deep emotion which thrills the hearts of those great artists who – at the height of their youthful love for art – come across a genius or some masterpiece. All human feelings reveal an early flowering, born from the most noble enthusiasm, which little by little fades away, until all that remains of happiness is a mem-ory and glory is but a lie. None of our fragile emotions is closer to love than the new-born passion of an artist experiencing for the first time the agonising ecstasy of his glorious and miser-able destiny, a passion replete with boldness and diffidence, with vague beliefs and the certainty of regularly losing heart. The youth who – penniless and not yet full grown in genius – has never felt his heart throb in the presence of a master, will always lack a chord in his heart, a certain touch of the brush, feeling in the work, a particular poetry of expression. Brag-garts swollen with their own image and precociously confident of the future are wise men only in the eyes of fools. For his part, the unknown youth appeared to possess real merit if the measure of talent is that initial shyness, that ineffable modesty those who are bound for glory learn to lose in the exercise of

9

their art, as pretty women lose theirs when they deploy the stratagems of coquetry. The habit of triumph conquers doubt, and what is modesty if not doubt?

Overcome with worries and astonished at this moment by his own effrontery, the poor neophyte would not have brought himself to enter the studio of the painter to whom we owe the splendid portrait of Henri IV, if chance had not come to his aid in an extraordinary way. An old man suddenly came up the stairs. From the bizarre nature of this individual's dress, from the magnificence of his lace collar, from the self-confidence of his bearing, the young man guessed he was either a patron or friend of the painter and stepped back on the landing to allow him to pass; meanwhile he looked him over with curiosity, hoping to discover in the old man the good nature of an artist or the obliging character of those who love the arts; but there was something diabolical in that face and on top of that a quality of *mystery* bound to attract any artist. Imagine a bald, curved and prominent forehead, jutting out over a small flattened nose, turned up at the end like Rabelais' or Socrates'; a wrinkled laughing mouth; a short chin proudly held up, covered with a grey pointed beard; sea-green eyes apparently dimmed by age but which through their contrast with the mother-of-pearl whites in which the eyeballs floated must sometimes throw magnetic glances when fired by anger or enthusiasm. The face too was strangely withered by the weariness of old age, and even more by those thoughts which dig deep into soul and body alike. The eyes no longer had any lashes and there was only the merest trace of eyebrows visible above their prominent arches. Place this head on a thin and feeble body, surround it with shining white lace wrought like a fish slice, throw in a heavy gold chain over the old man's doublet, and you have a faint idea of this individual who took on an even more fantastical dimension in the imperfect light of the staircase: a Rembrandt walking slowly, outside its frame, in the dark atmosphere eternally associated with that great painter. He cast a wise glance over the younger man, knocked three times on the door and said to the sickly-looking man of around forty who opened it: 'Good morning, master.'

Porbus bowed respectfully and, thinking the young man was accompanying the older visitor, allowed him in; and any doubts he might have had about him ceased at the sight of the neophyte, like all true-born painters, falling under the spell of an artist's studio, in which some of the material processes of art reveal themselves to him for the first time. An opened

10

window in the roof supplied the light for the studio of Master Porbus. Concentrated upon an easel with a canvas so far bearing only three or four white strokes, the daylight did not reach into the black depths and corners of that vast room; but a few stray shafts of light were reflected in the brown shade from the silvered spangle in the midriff of a horseman's breastplate hanging on the wall, sharply set off the waxed and carved cornice of an antique sideboard filled with curious plates and dishes, and pointed up the bright grained weft of some ancient gold brocaded curtains with great torn folds lying around as models. Anatomical statuettes in plaster, fragments and torsos of antique goddesses, lovingly polished by the kisses of time over the centuries, lay strewn about the consoles and shelves. Countless sketches in red chalk or ink, studies in black, red and white crayon on tinted paper, covered the walls from floor to ceiling. He squeezed his way between boxes of colours, bottles of oil and essences, and overturned stools, to arrive under the aureole projected by the rays from the high window which flooded the pale face of Porbus and the ivory skull of the strange old man. Soon the young man's attention was caught exclusively by a picture which, in this time of trouble and revolutions, had already become famous and had been visited by some of those stubborn men who keep the sacred flame alive during dark times. This beautiful canvas was a representation of Saint Mary the Egyptian about to pay for her boat journey to Palestine. This masterpiece, destined for Marie de Medici, was sold by her during the period of her poverty.

'I like your saint', the old man said to Porbus, 'and I would give you ten gold crowns more for her than the queen is paying. But compete with the queen? I'm damned if I will!'

'So you think she's quite good?'

'Hm', said the old man. 'Quite good? Well, yes and no. Your good woman is not badly got up, but there's no life in her. You all think you've done what needs to be done when you've drawn a face correctly and put everything in the proper place according to the laws of anatomy! You colour this or that feature with a flesh tone mixed in advance on your palette, taking care to make one side darker than the other; and because from time to time you look at a naked woman standing on a table you think you've succeeded in copying nature, you imagine yourselves to be painters and you fancy you have stolen God's secret from him! . . . Ha! To be a great poet it is not enough to know your syntax to perfection and to avoid grammatical errors. Look at your saint, Porbus. At first glance she

11

seems wonderful. But a second look reveals that she is stuck to the background of the painting and that one couldn't walk around her. She is a silhouette with one side to her only, a figure cut out, an image which cannot turn around, cannot change position. I am not conscious of any air between that arm and the ground of the picture; space and depth are lacking; yet the perspective is correctly done and the gradation of light and shade exactly observed: but despite these praiseworthy efforts I find it impossible to believe that the warm breath of life animates this beautiful body. It seems to me that if I were to place my hand on the firmly rounded throat, I would find it as cold as marble! No, my friend, blood does not flow beneath this ivory skin, the crimson dew of life does not swell the network of veins and capillaries intertwining beneath the amber transparency of her temples and breast. Here is life, movement – there only stillness; in every piece life and death struggle with each other: here is a woman, there is a statue, there again a corpse. Your creation is unfinished. You were able to breathe only a portion of your soul into your cherished work. The torch of Prometheus has gone out more than once in your hands, and many parts of your picture have not been touched by the celestial flame.

'But what is the reason for this, my dear master?', asked Porbus respectfully, while the young man had some difficulty in repressing his strong desire to thrash the old one.

'The reason? Well', said the little old man, 'in two minds you have fluctuated between the two systems, between drawing and colour, between the stolid thoroughness, the stiff precision of the old German masters, and the radiant fervour, the joyous abundance of the Italian painters. You sought to imitate at one and the same time Holbein and Titian, Albrecht Dürer and Paul Veronese. That was a truly magnificent ambition! But where has it led you? You have achieved neither the severe charm of dryness nor the magical deceptions of *chiaroscuro*. Here, for example, like molten bronze bursting through a fragile mould, the rich golden colouring of the Titian has torn asunder the thin outlines of Dürer into which you poured it. Elsewhere the contours have resisted and thwarted the magnificent outpourings of the Venetian palette. Your face is neither perfectly drawn nor perfectly painted, and all over it we can see the traces of your wretched indecision. If you did not feel strong enough to fuse the two rival manners in the fire of your own genius, you should have opted frankly for one or the other, in order to obtain the unity which simulates one of the conditions of life. What you have created is true only in the centres; your outlines are false, too disconnected, and give no promise of anything behind. There is some truth here, said the old man, pointing to the breast of the saint. Here too, he continued, signalling the point in the picture where the shoulder finished. But there, he said, coming back to the centre of the throat, everything is false. Let's stop analysing, you will only despair.'

The old man sat down on a stool and, silent, held his head between his hands.

'Yet I studied that throat from life, dear master', Porbus said to him, 'but to our great misfortune there are effects which however real in nature look most improbable on canvas.'

'The mission of art is not to copy nature but to express it! You're a poet, not some paltry copyist!', the old man exclaimed brusquely, interrupting Porbus with a despotic gesture. 'Otherwise the work of a sculptor would be done if he made a cast of the woman modelling for him! Well, try casting the hand of your mistress: when you study it you will find you have a horrible corpse before you, bearing no resemblance to the living hand, and you will have no choice but to go and find the chisel of the man who, without making an exact copy of the hand, will fashion for you its movement and its life. We have to seize the spirit, the soul, the very face of things and beings. Effects! effects! These are the accidents of life, not life itself. A hand, since I have already taken that example, a hand does not belong only to the body, it expresses and continues a thought which must be seized and rendered. Neither painter nor poet nor sculptor must separate effect from cause, which are bound up ineluctably together. This is the ground of the real struggle. Many painters in their work triumph instinctively without ever understanding what the subject of art is. You draw a woman, but you do not really see her! That is not the way to force nature to give up her secrets. Without any conscious thought your hand reproduces the model you copied in your master's studio. You do not go intimately or deeply enough into form, you do not pursue it – through all its flights and detours – with enough love and perseverance. Beauty is a thing severe and difficult of access which does not allow itself to be attained in that way. You have to await the right moment, spy her out, press her and grasp her tightly to force her to surrender. Form is a Proteus much more elusive and fertile in its folds than the Proteus of legend, and only after long battles can it be persuaded to reveal itself in its true colours; there are those who

13

are quite content with the first aspect it presents, at most with the second or third; this is not the way victorious fighters carry on! Undefeated painters do not allow themselves to be fooled by all those shifts; they persevere until nature is forced to lay herself bare and stand revealed in her truest spirit. That was how Raphael worked', said the old man removing his black velvet hat as an expression of the respect inspired in him by the king of art, 'his greatness and superiority derive from the inmost sense which, in him, seems intent on bursting the form. In his faces, form – as with us – is a dragoman to spread ideas, sensations; it is the grandest poetry. Every face contains a world, a portrait whose model appeared for him in a sublime vision, tinged with light, signalled by an inner voice, laid bare by a heavenly figure which revealed the sources of expression in the past of a whole life. You give your women beautiful robes of flesh, beautiful draperies of hair, but where is the blood which engenders serenity or passion, and which causes particular effects? Your saint is supposed to be a dark lady but this part here, my poor friend, is rather on the fair side, no? You parade your figures, these pale-coloured phantoms, before our eyes, and you call that painting, you call that art. Just because you've made something which looks more like a woman than a house you think you have attained your goal; and proud of no longer having to write *currus venustus* or *pulcher homo* beside your figures, as the early painters did, you consider yourselves to be fabulous artists! Ha! you are mighty fine fellows but fabulous artists you are not, not yet anyway. You will have to use up many crayons, cover many canvases, before you reach that point. Undoubtedly a woman carries her head this way, gathers her skirts like that; her eyes grow languid and melt with that air of sweet resignation; the flickering shadow of her eyelashes floats thus upon her cheeks! It is that and it is not that. What is missing? Nothing. But that nothing is everything. You have caught the appearance of life but you are not expressing its fullness and the way the fullness overflows, that enigmatic quality which cannot be described and which is the soul perhaps and which wanders like a cloud on the surface, in a word – that flower of life Titian and Raphael took by surprise. If you were to take off at the ultimate point where you come to rest, you would perhaps create an excellent painting; but you grow weary too soon. The common people look on amazed, while the real connoisseur smiles. Oh Mabuse, oh my master', added this strange individual, 'you are a thief, you stole away with life! All the same,' he went on,

14

'this canvas is worth more than all the paintings of that cad Rubens, with his mountains of Flemish meat sprinkled with vermillion, his showers of red hair, his din of colour. At least in your work colour, feelings and line, the three essential elements in art, complement each other.'

'But my good fellow, the saint is sublime', the young man – emerging from a deep reverie – cried in a loud voice. 'There is an intended subtlety about these two figures, the saint and the boatman, which you don't find in the Italian masters. I can't think of one who could have managed the hesitation of the boatman.'

'The little scamp! Does he belong to you by any chance?' Porbus asked the old man.

'I'm sorry, master. Forgive my boldness', replied the neophyte, blushing. 'I'm unknown, a dauber by instinct, lately arrived in this city which is the source of all knowledge.'

'To work', said Porbus, handing him a piece of red chalk and a sheet of paper.

The unknown nimbly sketched the saint in outline.

'Aha!', cried the old man. 'What is your name?'

The young man wrote *Nicolas Poussin* at the bottom of the sketch.

'It's not bad for a beginner', said the curious individual who had been discoursing so wildly. 'I see we can talk painting in your presence. I do not blame you for admiring Porbus's saint. To the world she is a masterpiece, and only those initiated into the deepest mysteries of art can discover where she is at fault. But since you are worthy of the lesson, and well able to understand it, I am going to show you how little is needed to complete this work. You must be all eyes and attention, another opportunity to instruct you may never present itself again. Your palette, Porbus?'

Porbus went to fetch his palette and brushes. Brusquely, convulsively, the old man rolled up his sleeves, fixed his thumb in the tinted and speckled palette which Porbus handed him, grabbed rather than took from the latter's hands a fistful of brushes of every size; and then there was a sudden and threatening movement of his pointed beard, expressing the itch of a lover's fantasy. As he dipped his brush, he muttered between his teeth: 'these colours are fit only to be chucked out of the window together with their perpetrator: they're crude and false, disgusting! How could anyone paint with them?' Then with feverish excitement he dipped the point of the brush into the different heaps of colour, often running the gamut more rapidly than a cathedral organist playing the *O Filii* hymn on his keyboard at Easter.

Porbus and Poussin stood motionless, one on each side, lost in the most vehement contemplation of the canvas.

'You see, youngster', said the old man without turning round, 'you see how with three or four brush strokes and a bluish glaze the air could be said to circulate around the head of this poor saint who must have felt stifled and trapped in the close atmosphere! See how this drapery is now fluttering and how one senses the breeze lifting it! Before, she seemed like a piece of canvas, stiff and supported by pins. Notice how the satin sheen which I have just given the breast is an appropriate rendering of the lithe softness of a young girl's skin and how the mixed tone of red brown and burnt ochre warms up the dull coldness of this deep shadow where the blood froze instead of flowing freely. Young man, young man, what I am showing you here no master could teach you. Mabuse alone possessed the secret of breathing life into figures. Mabuse had only one pupil, me. I have had none, and I am old. You have enough intelligence to guess the rest from these glimpses I am allowing you.'

While the strange old man was speaking, he put touches to all parts of the picture: here two strokes of the brush, there just one, yet always so absolutely right you would have thought you were facing a new picture, but a picture bathed in light. He worked so passionately, with such ardour, that pearls of sweat drenched his bare head. He made such rapid, impatient and jerky movements that to the young Poussin it seemed as though there was a demon in the body of this bizarre individual which was operating through his hands and making them work in a fantastic way, against his will. The supernatural sparkle in his eyes, the convulsions which seemed to be the result of some kind of resistance gave this idea a semblance of truth which was guaranteed to have an effect on a youthful imagination. The old man continued, saying: 'slap bang, slap bang, that's the way to lay it on, young man! Come, my little touches, warm these icy tones! Come on, boom, boom, boom', and he heated up those parts he had earlier signalled as lacking in life by applying layers of colour which abolished the disparities due to the artist's temperament and regained the unity of tone required by an ardent Egyptian.

'You see, young fellow, its the last stroke only which counts. Porbus made a hundred. I made one. No one will thank us for what is underneath. That is something you should know.'

16

At last the demon stopped, and turning to Porbus and Poussin who stood there breathless with admiration, said: 'it's still nowhere near my Catherine Lescault, but one could put one's name to it. Yes, I would sign it!', he added, rising to pick up a mirror in which he looked at the saint. 'Now let's go and have some lunch. I've got some smoked ham and good wine! Heh, heh, the times may be difficult, but we can still talk shop! and on equal terms. This boy has real talent', he said, placing his hand on the shoulder of Nicolas Poussin. As he made this gesture he noticed the young Norman's shabby cloak.

The old man took a leather purse out of his belt, searched in it, found two gold coins and offered them to Poussin. 'I'll buy your drawing', he said. 'Go on, take it', insisted Porbus, seeing him start and blush with shame, for the young disciple had a poor man's pride. 'Take it, he's got two kings' ransoms in his pouch!'

The three came down together from the studio and, as they walked along the street, talked about art. Eventually they reached a fine wooden house close to the Pont Saint-Michel. Its ornaments, knocker, window frames and arabesques all amazed Poussin. All of a sudden the would-be painter found himself in a low-ceilinged room, in front of a good fire, beside a table laden with tasty dishes and, through his unheard-of good fortune, in the company of two great and good-natured artists. 'Young man', said Porbus, seeing him open-mouthed before a picture, 'do not look at it for too long, you will only fall prey to despair.'

It was the *Adam* Mabuse painted to buy himself out of prison where his creditors had enforced a lengthy stay. The figure presented such a powerful embodiment of reality that Nicolas Poussin from that moment began to understand the true meaning of the confused words spoken by the old man. The latter looked at the picture with an air of satisfaction, but without enthusiasm, as if to say: I have done better than that. 'There is life in it', he said. 'My poor master surpassed himself in this. But some part of truth is still lacking in the background. The man is alive, he stands up and is about to walk towards us. But the air, the sky, the wind we breathe, see and feel, are missing. So far there is nothing but a man there! Now, the only man who came straight from God's hands must have something divine about him – which is missing here. Mabuse said so himself with vexation, when he wasn't drunk.'

Poussin looked at both men in turn, with curiosity and anxiety. He went up to Porbus as if to ask him the name of their host but the painter put his finger to his lips with an air of mystery and the young man, fascinated, kept his peace, hoping that sooner or later something might be said which would enable him to divine the name of this man whose wealth and talent were sufficiently attested by the respect Porbus showed him, and by the treasures overflowing in the room.

Poussin, seeing the magnificent portrait of a woman on the dark oak panelling, cried out 'what a wonderful Giorgione!'

'No', replied the old man, 'you're looking at one of my early daubs.'

'God in heaven, I am in the house of the god of painting', said the Poussin naively.

The old man smiled like one long familiar with such praise. 'Master Frenhofer', said Porbus, 'won't you bring me up some of your excellent Rhine wine?'

'Two casks', replied the old man. 'One to reciprocate the pleasure I had this morning when I saw your pretty little sinner, the other as a present from a friend.'

'Ah, if I weren't always ill', replied Porbus, 'and if you would only let me see your *mistress*. I could paint a picture high and wide and deep, with life-size figures.'

'Show you my work', the painter cried with emotion. 'No, no, I have still not perfected it. Yesterday, as night approached, I thought I had finished. Her eyes seemed moist, her flesh was restless. You could see movement in the tresses of her hair. She was breathing! Although I had found the means of realising on a flat canvas the relief and roundness of nature, this morning, in the light, I discovered my error. Ah, to come to such a glorious pass, I studied in depth the great masters of colouring, I analysed – removing layer after layer – the paintings of Titian, that king of light; I have, like that sovereign painter, sketched out my figure in a clear tone with a supple thick-laid impasto, for shadow is but an accident of light, take that in youngster. Then I went back over my work, and by means of half-tints and glazes whose transparency I diminished in stages, I created the most vigorous shadows and the deepest of blacks; for the shadows of ordinary painters are of a completely different nature from their high-lights; they are wood or brass or what you will, anything but flesh in shadow. One feels that if a figure changed position the place of its shadow would not grow clean and luminous. I have avoided this error, into which some of the most illustrious painters have fallen, and in my work whiteness shines through the opacity of the most deeply sustained shadow. Unlike that

18

mass of ignoramuses who imagine they can draw correctly because their line is oh so cleanly defined I have not marked the outlines of my figure badly nor have I brought into relief the minutest anatomical details, for the human body is not bound by lines. In this respect sculptors can get closer to the truth than painters. Nature consists of a succession of rounded forms enveloping each other. Strictly speaking drawing does not exist! Don't laugh, young man! However peculiar my thought may seem to you, one day you will understand the reasoning behind it. Line is the method by which man realises the effect of light upon objects; but there are no lines in nature, where everything is rounded: we draw by modelling, that is to say we detach things from their setting, the distribution of light alone supplies the visual appearance of the body. Therefore I have not clearly highlighted individual features, but spread over the outlines a haze of warm and golden half-tints which mean you cannot place your finger on the exact place where the background and contours meet. From close up the work seems fuzzy and lacking definition, but take two steps back and the whole thing consolidates itself, acquires its own space and stands out; the body can turn round, the forms become prominent, you feel the air circulating. However, still I am not happy, still I have my doubts. Perhaps I should not draw one single line, perhaps it would be better to attack a figure from the middle by applying oneself first to the most prominently illumined parts, proceeding thereafter to darker areas. Is this not the method of the sun, the divine painter of the universe. Oh! nature, nature!, who has ever surprised you in your flights? Too much knowledge, like ignorance, ends up in a negation. I have the deepest doubts about my own work.'

The old man paused, then took up his theme again: 'I've been working on it for ten years, young man; but what are ten short years when we are talking about a struggle with Nature? We don't know how long it took Pygmalion to create the only statue that ever walked!'

The old man fell into a deep reverie and stared fixedly into the distance while playing mechanically with his knife.

'Look, he is conversing with his *spirit*', said Porbus in a low voice.

Hearing this, Nicolas Poussin felt himself in that inexplicable grip, an artist's curiosity. For him the white-eyed old man, at once alert and foolish, had become something more than a man, a fantastical spirit living in an unknown region. A thousand confused ideas were waking in his soul. The mental

19

phenomenon of this kind of fascination can no more be defined than one can translate the emotion caused in the heart of an exile by a song recalling his homeland. The old man's expressed contempt for the most beautiful artistic endeavours, his wealth, his manners, the deference shown by Porbus, this work of his kept secret for so long, this work born of patience, work doubtless of genius, judging by the virgin's head the young Poussin had so openly admired and which, beautiful even in comparison with Mabuse's *Adam*, attested to the imperial technique of a prince of art: everything about this old man went beyond the limits of human nature. What was clearly perceptible to the rich imagination of Nicolas Poussin as he regarded this supernatural being, was a complete image of the nature of artists, that crazy nature to which so many powers are entrusted and which too often abuses them, leading cold reason, bourgeois types and even some experts over a thousand stony paths to a place where, for them, there is nothing; while playful in her every whim, nature, that white-winged girl, discovers epics there, castles and works of art. Nature mocking and kind-hearted, fecund and barren! Thus, for the enthusiastic Poussin the old man had, in a sudden transfiguration, become art itself, art with its secrets, its passions, its reveries.

'Yes, my dear Porbus', continued Frenhofer, 'so far I have failed to make the acquaintance of a faultless woman, a body whose contours are of the utmost beauty and perfection, and whose colouring. . . . but where can she be found in this life', he said interrupting himself, 'that beautiful lost Venus of the ancients, sought so often, and of whom we only and rarely come upon some scattered fragments? Oh to see her at last, just once, for one brief moment, this nature divine and complete, the Ideal, I would give my entire fortune, yes I would seek you in your limbo, celestial beauty! Like Orpheus I shall go down into the hell of art, to bring life back from there.'

'It's time to leave now', said Porbus to Poussin. 'He can't hear us any more, he can't see us any more!'

'Let's go up to his studio', replied the amazed youth.

'Oh, the crafty old fellow has made sure no one can get in. His treasures are too well guarded for us to be able to see them. I didn't wait for your suggestion, for your fancy, before mounting my own assault on this mystery.'

'Then there is mystery?'

'Yes', replied Porbus. 'Old Frenhofer is the only pupil Mabuse was willing to take on. Frenhofer became his friend, his saviour and his father, and sacrificed the greater part of his fortune to enable Mabuse to satisfy his passions; in return, Mabuse bequeathed him the secret of relief, the power of endowing his figures with that extraordinary life, that flower of nature, which is our ever-present despair, but whose technique Mabuse possessed in such a thoroughgoing way that one day when he had sold and drunk the proceeds of the flowered damask coat he was to wear at the reception of Charles Quint, he accompanied his master in a paper coat he had painted to resemble the real thing. The peculiarly flamboyant impact of the material worn by Mabuse surprised the emperor who, wanting to compliment the old drunkard's patron on the coat, discovered the deception. Frenhofer is full of intense passion for our art and sees higher and further than other artists. He has meditated profoundly on colour, on the absolute truth of line; but research has led him to doubt the very subject of that research. In moments of despair he claims that drawing does not exist and that all you can render with lines are geometrical figures; but this is too absolute a stance, since with line and with black – which is not a colour – you can indeed draw a human figure; which proves that our art, like nature itself, is composed of an infinite number of elements: drawing gives you the skeleton, colour brings it to life, but life without a skeleton is even more incomplete than a skeleton without life. Finally there is something even truer than all this, which is that practice and observation are the be-all and end-all for a painter, and that when reason and poetry come into conflict with your brushes you end up doubting yourself – like this good fellow, who is as much a madman as he is a painter. A sublime painter indeed, but who had the misfortune to be born rich, which has allowed him to stray. Do not imitate him! Work! Painters should only meditate brush in hand.'

'We *are* going to get in', cried Poussin, sublimely innocent and no longer hearing Porbus's words. Porbus smiled at the enthusiasm of the unknown youngster and, as he left, invited him to come again to his studio.

Nicolas Poussin returned slowly to rue de la Harpe and, without noticing, walked past the ancient hostelry where he was lodging. Then, anxiously, he hurried up the shabby staircase and reached an attic room situated beneath some half-timbering, that light and unaffected style of roof typical of the houses of old Paris. By the single gloomy window of the room could be seen a young girl. On hearing a noise at the door she suddenly stood up, her movement dictated by love;

21

she had recognised the painter by the way he tackled the latch.

'What is the matter?', she said to him.

'I . . . I . . .', he cried, choking with pleasure, 'at last I feel myself to be a painter! Till now I had doubts but this morning I finally believed in myself! I can be a great man! Wait and see, Gillette, we'll be rich, happy. There is gold in these brushes.'

But suddenly he fell silent. His face in all its vigour and gravity was drained of joy when he compared the immensity of his hopes with his mediocre resources. The walls were covered with crayon sketches on ordinary paper. He didn't even possess four clean canvases. Colours then were very expensive and this poor gentleman had an almost bare palette. Despite his wretched condition, he was conscious he possessed unbelievable riches of the heart, and the superabundance of an all-devouring genius. He had been brought to Paris by a well-to-do friend or perhaps by the promptings of his own talent, and had swiftly found a mistress, one of those noble and generous souls who choose to suffer by the side of a great man, espouse his troubles and learn to understand his whims; strong for him in poverty and love, as other women are intrepid in bearing the burden of luxury and parading their lack of sensitivity. The smile playing over Gillette's lips bathed the attic in gold and rivalled the brilliance of the heavens. The sun did not always shine, but Gillette was always there, gathered into her passion, attached to his happiness, his suffering, consoling the genius who overflowed with love before laying hands on his art.

'Listen, Gillette, come here.'

Obediently and joyously the girl climbed onto the painter's knee. She was all grace, all beauty, pretty as springtime, adorned with all the riches of the fair sex, and illuminating them with the fire of a beautiful soul.

'Oh God', he cried out, 'I'll never dare say it . . .'.

'A secret? I want to know'.

The Poussin was lost in his dream.

'Come on, tell me.'

'Gillette, poor dear heart!'

'Oh, so you want something of me?'

'Yes.'

'Listen, if you want me to sit for you again as I did the other day', she continued with a little pout, 'I shall never agree to it, for at those moments your eyes no longer speak to me, you stop thinking about me, even though you're looking at me.'

22

'Would you prefer it if I drew another woman?'

'Perhaps', she replied, 'if she were very ugly.'

'Well then', said the Poussin seriously, 'for the sake of my future glory, to make me a great painter, what if it were essential for you to sit for another painter?'

'You're trying to put me to the test', she said. 'You know I would never do it.'

The Poussin rested his head on her breast like a man overwhelmed by a grief or joy too strong for his soul.

'Listen, Nick', she said, pulling at the sleeve of his threadbare doublet. 'I told you I would give my life for you: but I never promised you I would renounce my love while I live.'

'Renounce it?', exclaimed Poussin.

'If I displayed myself in this way to another you would no longer love me. And as for me I would feel myself unworthy of you. Obeying your whims is the most natural and simplest thing in the world. Despite myself I am happy and even proud to do your will, my dear. But for another? Never.'

'Forgive me, my Gillette,' said the painter, falling on his knees. 'Your love is more important to me than glory. You are more beautiful than all the wealth and honour in the world. Throw away my brushes. Burn my sketches. I have made a mistake. My vocation is to love you. I am not a painter. I am a lover. Perish art and all its secrets.'

How she admired him! She was happy, enchanted: she was a queen, and felt instinctively that the arts were forgotten for her sake and thrown like grains of incense at her feet.

'And yet he's only an old man', continued Poussin. 'He will see only the female form in you, you are so perfect.'

'One must love well', she cried, ready to give up her scruples in love to compensate her lover for all the sacrifices he was making for her. 'But', she said, 'it would be the end of me. Ah, to ruin myself for you. Yes, that would be very fine. But you will forget me. Oh what a terrible thought you have had there.'

'Yes I did have it, and I love you', he said with something like contrition; 'I've been vile.'

'Should we consult Father Hardouin?', she said.

'Oh no, let it be a secret between us.'

'All right, I will do it. But you must not be there. Stay at the door, with your dagger ready. If I call, run in and kill the painter.'

With eyes only for his art, the Poussin held Gillette tightly in his arms.

23

'He no longer loves me', thought Gillette, when she was alone.

She already repented her decision. But soon she fell prey to a terror even more cruel than her repentance, and forced herself to chase away a dreadful thought which arose in her heart: she believed she already loved the painter less, suspecting he was now less praiseworthy.

II

CATHERINE LESCAULT

Three months after the meeting between Poussin and Porbus, the latter paid a visit to Master Frenhofer. Around this time the old man had fallen prey to one of those profound and spontaneous depressions caused – if we are to believe the medical mathematicians – by a bad digestion, by heat, by the wind, by a thickening of the hypochondrium; or, following the spiritualists, by the imperfection of our moral nature. The good man had purely and simply worn himself out perfecting his mysterious picture. He was languishing in a huge black leather chair of carved oak and, without abandoning his melancholy disposition, gave Porbus the look of a man who was well settled into his ennui.

'Well master', Porbus said to him, 'was the ultramarine you got from Bruges all that bad? Have you had any problems grinding the new white? Is your oil misbehaving? Are your brushes proving stubborn?'

'Alas', cried the old man, 'for a brief moment I thought I had completed my work; but I am certain I have made some mistakes of detail and I shall not rest until I have thrown light on them. I have made up my mind to travel and shall go to Turkey, to Greece, to Asia – for the purpose of finding a model and comparing my picture to diverse types from nature. Perhaps', he said, allowing himself a smile of contentment, 'perhaps nature herself is upstairs. Sometimes I am almost afraid that a single breath will awaken her and she will escape.' Then he rose suddenly, as if to leave.

'Aha', replied Porbus, 'I have come in time to save you the expense and exhaustion of the journey.'

'What', said Frenhofer in amazement.

'Young Poussin is loved by a woman of incomparable beauty, absolutely perfect. But, dear master, if he agrees to lend her to you, at the very least you must let us see your canvas.'

The old man stood motionless, in a state of complete stupefaction. 'What', he said at last, desolately. 'Show you my creature, my bride? Tear aside the veil beneath which I have chastely covered my pride and joy? That would be prostitution, horrible! I have lived with this woman for ten years, she is mine, mine alone, she loves me. Has she not smiled at me with every stroke of the brush I have given her? She has a soul, the soul I endowed her with. She would blush if eyes other than mine were to come to rest on her. Allow her to be seen? But where is the husband, the lover, so base as to lead his loved one to dishonour? When you paint a picture for the court, you don't put your entire soul into it, you sell the courtiers nothing but highly coloured marionettes! My painting is no painting. It is a sentiment, a passion! Born in my studio, she must remain there virgin, and only emerge fully clothed. Poetry and women reveal themselves naked only to their lovers. Do we possess Raphael's model? Ariosto's Angelica? Dante's Beatrice? No, we see their forms, that's all. Well, the work I keep under lock and key upstairs is an exception in our art. It is not a canvas, it is a woman! I weep with her, I laugh with her, I converse with her, I think with her. Would you have me discard ten years of happiness on the spur of the moment, like an old cloak? All at once cease being father, lover, God? This woman is not a creature, she is a creation. Let your young man come and visit. He can have my treasures, pictures by Correggio, Michelangelo, Titian; I shall kiss his footprints in the dust; but make him my rival? Shame on me! I am more of a lover still than I am painter. Yes, I shall have the strength to burn my Catherine when I breathe my last; but force her to endure the gaze of a man, a young man, a painter? No, no! The next day I would kill whoever sullied her with so much as a glance! And you, my friend, I would kill you on the spot if you did not salute her on your bended knees! Now, do you still want me to submit my idol to the cold eyes and critical stupidities of imbeciles? Ah, love is a mystery, it lives only in the depths of the heart, and all is lost when a man says, even to his best friend: that is the woman I love.'

The old man seemed to have become rejuvenated; there was ardour and life in his eyes; his pale cheeks were tinged with a vivid red, and his hands were trembling. Porbus, astonished by the violent passion with which the words were uttered, had not the faintest idea how to reply to a feeling as novel as it was profound. Was Frenhofer sane or mad? Was he in the grip of an artist's fantastication, or were the ideas he had expressed issuing from the inexpressible fanaticism produced in us by the long gestation of a great work of art? Could one ever hope to reach a compromise with such a bizarre passion?

With all these thoughts preying on his mind, Porbus said to

the old man: 'Is it not a fair exchange? After all, Poussin is allowing you to gaze upon his mistress.'

'Mistress?', replied Frenhofer. 'She'll betray him sooner or later. Mine will always be faithful to me.'

'All right', said Porbus, 'let's not talk about it any more. But before finding, even in Asia, a woman as beautiful, as perfect, you may die without having completed your picture.'

'Ah! it is finished', said Frenhofer. 'Whoever saw it would believe he was observing a woman lying on a velvet couch, beneath the surrounding curtains. Beside her, on a golden tripod, perfumes are burning. You would be tempted to grasp the tassle of the cords which hold back the curtains, and you would be sure you had seen the movement of Catherine's breast as she breathed. But I should still want to be absolutely certain . . .'

'Then go to Asia', replied Porbus, glimpsing some kind of hesitation in Frenhofer's look. And Porbus took a few steps in the direction of the door.

At that moment Nicolas Poussin and Gillette had arrived at the entrance to Frenhofer's house. As the young girl was about to enter she removed her arm from the painter's, and stepped back as if she had been seized by a sudden foreboding.

'What am I doing here', she asked her lover in a low voice, looking him straight in the eye.

'Gillette, it is up to you. I want to obey you in everything. You are my conscience and my glory. Go back home. I shall be happier, perhaps, than if you . . .'

'Do I have any control over my actions when you speak to me like that? No, I'm just a child. Come', she added, seemingly with a violent effort. 'If our love perishes, if life-long regret takes root in my heart, will not your fame be the reward for my obedience to your desires? Let's go in, it will be a sort of life to be an eternal memory upon your palette.'

As they walked through the gate of the house, the two lovers bumped into Porbus. Gillette's beauty caught him by surprise. She was trembling all over and her eyes by now were full of tears. Porbus brought her into the presence of the old man.

'Take a good look at her. Isn't she worth all the masterpieces in the world?'

Frenhofer gave a start. Gillette stood there, simple and ingenuous, like an innocent and nervous Georgian girl carried off by brigands and offered to some slave merchant. A chaste blush coloured her face, she lowered her eyes, her hands hung

27

by her sides, her strength seemed to have failed her, and her tears protested against the violence done to her modesty. At this moment Poussin cursed himself in his despair at having brought this fine treasure out of his attic. The lover in him conquered the artist, and a thousand scruples tortured his heart when he saw the old man's rejuvenated eye undress, so to speak – as painters do – the young girl, and guess the secrets of her curves and shapes. At this he reverted to the ferocious jealousy of real love.

'Let us go, Gillette', he cried.

Hearing his words and immediately affected by his tone of voice, the joyous mistress raised her eyes to him, looked hard at him, and ran into his arms. 'Ah you do love me', she cried, and dissolved into tears. Though she had found the energy to suppress her suffering, she lacked strength to hide her joy.

'Oh leave her alone with me for a few moments', said the old painter, 'and you shall compare her to my Catherine. Yes, I consent.'

There was love yet in Frenhofer's cry. He seemed to be flirting with his simulacrum of a woman, and enjoying in advance the triumph of the beauty of his virgin over that of a real girl.

'Hurry, don't let him change his mind', exclaimed Porbus, striking Poussin on the shoulder. 'The fruits of love pass quickly away, the fruits of art live on forever.'

'Am I therefore nothing more than a woman in his eyes?', replied Gillette, looking closely at Poussin and Porbus.' Proudly she raised her head and then, after flashing a glance at Frenhofer, saw her lover deep in contemplation again of the portrait he had formerly taken for a Giorgione. 'Ah', she said, 'let's go upstairs. He never looked at *me* that way.'

'Old man', said Poussin, plucked from his meditation by Gillette's voice, 'see this blade, I shall plunge it into your heart at the first cry from the girl. I shall set your house on fire and no one will leave it alive. Do you understand?'

Nicolas Poussin had a black look on his face; the terrible way he spoke, his attitude, his gesture, all were a kind of consolation for Gillette who almost forgave him for sacrificing her to painting and to his glorious future. Porbus and Poussin stood at the door of the studio and looked at each other in silence. At first the painter of Marie the Egyptian permitted himself some comments: 'Ah, she is undressing! He is telling her to stand in the light! He is making the comparison!' But he quickly shut up when he noticed the deep sadness on Poussin's face; and

28

although old painters no longer trouble with such petty scruples in the presence of art, Porbus admired their naive and beautiful form in the young man. Poussin gripped the hilt of his dagger firmly and his ear was almost glued to the door. The two men, as they stood in the shadow, resembled two conspirators awaiting the hour to strike a tyrant down.

'Come in, come in', said the old man to them, glowing with delight. 'My work is perfect, and now I can show her with pride. Never shall painter, brushes, colours, canvas and light rival Catherine Lescault!'

Possessed by the most intense curiosity, Porbus and Poussin hurried into the chaos of his vast and dust-ridden studio. Here and there they noticed pictures hanging on the walls. At first they stopped in admiration before the life-sized figure of a half-naked woman.

'Oh don't waste your time with that old canvas', said Frenhofer, 'I was messing about, studying a particular pose. The picture's worthless. These are my mistakes', he continued, pointing to the ravishing compositions hanging all round them.

Hearing this, Porbus and Poussin, flabbergasted by his disdain for work of such high quality – looked for the promised portrait, but could not find it anywhere.

'Well, here it is', the old man said to them. His hair was dishevelled, his face was animated by an extraordinary exaltation, his eyes sparkled, and he breathed like a love-intoxicated youth. 'Ah', he cried out, 'you never expected to witness so much perfection! A woman is facing you and you are looking for a picture. There is so much depth to that canvas, the air in there is so true that you cannot distinguish it from the air which surrounds us. Where is art? Lost, vanished! Those are the real curves of a young woman. Have I not caught to perfection the colour, the quick of the line which seems to encircle the body? Is it not the same phenomenon objects present to us in their own atmosphere, like fish in water? Admire the way the contours stand out from the background. Doesn't it seem as though you could pass your hand over the girl's back? To this end for seven whole years I studied the way objects and daylight merge into each other. And her hair, is it not drowned in light? She breathed! I'm sure. See, her breast! Ah, who would not fall to his knees breathless with adoration? All parts of her flesh are throbbing. She is about to stand up. Just wait and see.'

'Can you see anything?', Poussin asked Porbus.

29

'No. And you?'

'Nothing at all.'

The two painters left the old man to his ecstasy, and looked to see whether the light falling fully frontal on the canvas he was showing them had not perhaps neutralised all its effects. Then they went right up to the picture and examined it successively from the left, from the right, in front, kneeling down and standing up.

'Yes, yes, it's a canvas all right', said Frenhofer to them, misunderstanding the purpose of their detailed examination. 'See, here are the canvas frame, the easel, here my colours, my brushes.'

And he grabbed one of the brushes, which he handed to them with a naive gesture. 'The old warrior is playing games with us', said Poussin, returning to the supposed picture. 'I see nothing there but confused masses of colours contained by a multitude of strange lines, forming a high wall of paint.'

'We're wrong', said Porbus, 'look.'

Moving closer they noticed in the corner of the canvas the tip of a bare foot emerging from the chaos of colours, tones and vague hues, a shapeless fog; but it was a delicious foot, a living foot! They stood petrified with admiration before this fragment which had somehow managed to escape from an unbelievable, slow and progressive destruction. The foot seemed to them like the torso of some Venus in Parian marble rising from the ruins of a city destroyed by fire.

'There is a woman underneath', exclaimed Porbus, bringing to Poussin's attention the layers of colours which the old painter had successively superimposed in the belief he was perfecting his painting.

Both painters turned spontaneously towards Frenhofer as they began to understand, albeit vaguely, the ecstasy in which he lived.

'There is no doubt about his good faith', said Porbus.

'Yes, my friend', replied the old man, waking up: 'faith, you need faith, faith in art, and you have to live a long time with your work in order to produce such a creation. Some of these shadows cost me untold labour. Look, on her cheek, beneath the eyes, there is a faint penumbra which if you observed it in real life would appear to be almost untranslatable into paint. Well do you believe me now when I tell you that the reproduction of that shadow required the most extraordinary toil? What is more, my dear Porbus, if you look at my work attentively, you will understand better what I was telling you about how to treat relief and contours. Look closely at the light of the breast and see how, by a series of touched-in high-lights set in strong impastos, I have succeeded in catching the real light and working it in with the shining white of the lit tones; and how, with a contrary skill, effacing the juts and grain of the impasto, by dint of drowning the contours of my figure in kisses of half-tint, I have contrived to do away with the very idea of drawing and other artificial methods, and give her the rounded aspect of nature itself. Come closer. You will get a better view of this work; from afar it disappears. But here, look, it is very remarkable, in my opinion.' And with the tip of his brush he pointed out a patch of bright colour to the two painters.

Turning towards Poussin, Porbus placed his hand on the old man's shoulder and said to the young man: 'You do know that in him we see a very great painter?'

'He is even more poet than painter', Poussin replied gravely.

'Here', resumed Porbus, touching the canvas, 'here is the end of art on earth'.

'Henceforth it will lose itself in the heavenly spheres', said Poussin.

'What enjoyments there are upon that piece of canvas', exclaimed Porbus.

The old man, absorbed in himself, was not listening to them; he was smiling at his imaginary woman.

'But sooner or later he will discover there is nothing on his canvas', cried Poussin.

'Nothing on my canvas?', said Frenhofer, looking from one painter to the other, and then at the supposed picture.

'What have you done?', replied Porbus to Poussin.

The old man grasped forcibly the young man's arm and said to him: 'so you see nothing, you lout! you lubber! you bandit! you bumboy! What made you come up to my studio? Good Porbus', he said turning to the painter, 'are you making a fool of me too? Answer! I am your friend, tell me now, have I spoiled my picture?'

Porbus, hesitating, did not dare speak; but the anxiety portrayed on the old man's white face was so grievous that he pointed to the canvas and said: 'Look.'

Frenhofer briefly contemplated his picture and staggered back.

'Nothing! nothing! The work of ten years!' He sat down and wept. 'What a crazy old fool I am! I have neither talent nor capabilities, I am nothing but a rich man who,

31

while walking, can only walk. In the end I shall have done nothing!'

He contemplated his picture through his tears, then all of a sudden stood up proudly, and cast a flashing glance at the two painters.

'By the blood and by the body and by the head of Christ, you are both jealous, wanting to make me believe the picture is spoiled so you can steal it from me! I can see her', he cried. 'She is marvellously beautiful.'

At this moment Poussin heard Gillette weeping in a corner, forgotten.

'Oh what is it, my angel?', the painter asked her, transformed suddenly into a lover once again.

'Kill me', she said. 'I must be vile to continue loving you, for I despise you. You are my life and you fill me with loathing. I think I already hate you.'

While Poussin was listening to Gillette, Frenhofer draped a green serge cloth over his Catherine with the serious tranquillity of a jeweller who locks his drawers while suspecting his customers of being crafty thieves. He gave the two painters a profoundly cunning look, scornful, suspicious, and showed them to the door of his studio silently and with convulsive haste. Then on the threshold of his house he said to them: 'Farewell, my young friends.'

The words froze them. The next day, Porbus, full of anxiety, returned to Frenhofer's house, and learned that he had died during the night, after burning his pictures.

THE INTERROGATIVE
APPARITION

"You have to copy what you see, no? And at the same time you have to make a picture"
                           – Giacometti

"All painting appears therefore as an abortive effort to say something which always remains to be said"
                         – Merleau-Ponty

"It's not always easy to say which – the painting or the artist's talk about it – is the egg and which is the hen"
                         – Beckett

"Vissi d'arte, vissi d'amore"
                         – Tosca

A Reality of Semblance

Balzac's highly complex, endlessly fascinating and vertiginously brilliant text is the story of three men, painters, one of whom must die, and three women (two being paintings), one of whom must die. The tale is a diptych, each section named after a woman, one "real" – the young man's mistress and model – the other "painted" – the old man's virgin and mistress. The whole is preceded by an enigmatic dedication, 'To a Lord', whose dots may be emblematic of Balzac's intuitive design: a projection to and from the 17th century of the unknown (to Balzac though not to us) void which will be the long journey towards the art of the future, from Cézanne and impressionism through fauvism and analytical cubism to surrealism, abstract expressionism and action painting. 'I see nothing there but confused masses of colours contained by a multitude of strange lines, forming a high wall of paint' – this oft-quoted reaction by Poussin to Frenhofer's canvas has led many critics, painters and other readers to say, quite rightly, that there would be no problem today if it were displayed alongside work by de Kooning, Newman, Pollock and others. Poussin and Porbus understand they are faced with a closure, a closure which to them is the 'end of art on earth', a closure which thanks to Balzac's incandescent genius foreshadows the future of painting after his own time, a closure which on the other side of the (dotted) void is a beginning. One great twentieth century artist in particular appears to be anticipated: Giacometti.

The Unknown Masterpiece is a story of two geniuses, one embryonic, entering the universe of art/life, the other leaving it, and both mediated by a man of the world, important, famous, talented, but not a genius, save in his narrative function as the go-between. At the same time the story is told of three women, two saints who become whores by being displayed to the gaze (embrace, knowledge) of the other painter, and mediated by the third painter's woman, a painting of Mary of Egypt who was both saint *and* whore.

The story is so heavily over-determined in terms of the modalities of discourse by means of which one might attempt to read its telling closely – sex and love, poetry and painting, writing and painting, painting and life, knowledge and commerce, money and fame, myth and art, art and history – and yet so satisfyingly poised in its nervous tension and stable disequilibrium that this translator felt he had to go beyond his professional offering and investigate the story's complexities in an essay. We shall look to see what is going on in the story, and *see* is the operative word. Registers

35

available in disproportionate intensity to the greatest writers interlock in this short text; it is one of the most revised works of an author much given to revising. Image calls to image, phrase to phrase, syntactic element to syntactic element, rhythm to rhythm, the whole strung along two complex systems of exchange and a dialectic of the pictural and scriptural, with the characters' destiny manifest and incarnate in their own and the narrator's comments. The story is a collage of historical and legendary allusions, multiple mythological structures and theorising about art.

Balzac's tale incorporates, incarnates a network of myths. It also embodies a dual system of exchange, a triangle of men superimposed on a triangle of women but it is, oh dear yes, a love story, though Poussin is surely not as much in love as he and Balzac and we would like to think. It contains *all* the grand Romantic themes of love, death, art, religion, politics (ie, here, money), while its high seriousness and anxiety about art (social, psychological, technical and linguistic) is symptomatic and partly generative of that element in Romanticism which will culminate in symbolism and decadence. The crisis in artists' relationship to their own work, the disjunction between human subject matter and the way it is handled (Cézanne, Manet, etc) will lead to a hopeless pursuit of antique confidence and traditional reassurance but the pursuit, as the I Ching says, only makes the quarry run faster.

There cannot be many short texts which contain so many different and simultaneously implicit and explicit mythical allusions, not to mention lending themselves to additional ones. Frenhofer not only embodies all the named and unnamed mythic figures (described later in this essay), he is himself a myth, incarnating the elaboration and demystification of the historical situation of the romantic artist, involving money, autonomy and so on. The Renaissance model of the artist just about fits Porbus but cracks under the strain placed on it by the behaviour and attitudes of Poussin and Frenhofer. The crisis of confidence in Balzac's own day, the forthcoming alienation of the artist from the market, makes him nervous. To keep himself warm he feverishly lays it on thick (like Frenhofer), for the void he identifies, the void of the dedication and its time-warp, is very scary indeed, a cold and public place where a living hand would freeze. It is, after all, quite unusual to body forth the aesthetic morality of another artist (Giacometti) over a hundred years before that "rocher en mouvement" (in Picon's words), that "phénomène d'espérance" (Picon on Giacometti again but quoting Balzac on himself) begins his "obsession de la ressemblance" (Picon). So unusual indeed, that you cover your tracks, so as not to lose yourself in a lonely madness

– you are a visionary not a realist as Baudelaire was the first to emphasise.

What happens is that your story, written a few years before the first recorded modern use of the word "avant-garde" (1845), inspires and influences writers and artists of all kinds, many of whom misunderstand it (artists refusing to read the meanings of their behaviour and art-historians refusing to read the meanings of their language, as Audrey Jones has commented) for well over a hundred years, until the 1980s when quite a large literature, including whole books, appears on it. Can Frenhofer be lagging far behind Frankenstein in the popular mind? Answer, yes, so far. Ahead of its time like its exact contemporary, Büchner's *Lenz, The Unknown Masterpiece* is one of the supreme moments in nineteenth century literature.

On one level the story reveals the author's dialectically intuitive awareness that you do your work as an artist in a no-nonsense way, the way of your eventual reader who requires and deserves a shared discourse of social intelligibility, despite or perhaps because of the temptation to go over the top and to tumble into the madness so closely allied to that creative principle which is supposed to be the well-spring of the romantic artist in the first place. In a passage in one of his longest and greatest novels, *La Cousine Bette* (1846), Balzac warns all those tempted to go over the top including himself and, if you go by appearances and the arguments of many critics, Frenhofer: "if the artist does not precipitate himself into his work, if he contemplates the difficulties instead of resolving them one by one, his oeuvre remains incomplete, perishes in his studio, where production becomes impossible, and the artist assists at the suicide of his talent."

It is easy to forget when reading this story that its locus is neither the seventeenth nor the twentieth century, but the early nineteenth century. Beneath the layer of Romantic ideology about the solitary artist (perhaps the earliest portrait) lies the prophetic sub-text embedded and embodied in the story's deep structure: that for many artists achievement henceforth implies the central principle of anxiety/doubt/failure/incompletion/revision. Some of these artists will despair and die, others not. Can anyone familiar with the work and life of Cézanne and Giacometti fail to identify his/her reader's own hindsight with Balzac's authorial foresight or pre-cognition, fail to read these great and exemplary artists into and out of Balzac's story? (See pages 51–3 of this essay for more specific argument on them and on the special case of Washington Allston whom Frenhofer's third discourse irresistibly brings to mind.) They embark on a quest for the absolute – Sartre's name for

Giacometti's journey, taken from the title of Balzac's eponymous novel of 1834 which, like our story, is in the *Etudes philosophiques* – and they must, in some sense, fail. But, like Vladimir and Estragon, they pick up and go on. It is true that Balzac wrote to Madame de Hanska in the letter of May 24, 1837: "... the work and its execution killed by the over-abundance of the creative principle ... which dictated *The Unknown Masterpiece* to me in respect of painting"; and in the preface to *A Daughter of Eve* (1839), that *The Unknown Masterpiece* demonstrates "the laws which produce the suicide of art". And many major critics including Arnheim and Kermode share Balzac's declared view that this is a story of failure as such, whether due to hubris or idealism or madness, and is thus a warning. I believe that this is merely a secondary reading as are several others based on surface and static principles. One primary reading involves premonition of the necessity of (as-if) failure in the achievement of the highest art, achievement as *process*, which is *written through* the nervous energy of Frenhofer's discourses.

The view, shared by all critics until modern times as well as by Balzac and Frenhofer, that the painter/writer in the story is a failure, is destroyed not because the old man is in fact a success story, though we argue he is, but by the fact that he is given to doubt. Hubris does not admit of such doubt, or if it does it is still not the reason for the doubt: the sense of failure, the anxiety – these arise because they are built into his project. It is quite wonderful how the side of artistic creativity which Porbus and Balzac warn against (and with reason) should help to generate a hallucinatory premonition of Giacometti, the twentieth century's greatest and most exemplary artist. There is a true, famous, beautiful and Borges-like story that in one of his houses Balzac had written either on the wall or inside some empty frames: "(Here) Velasquez, (here) Delacroix, (here) Raphael" – quite a parable of a writer's felt life, and one would have liked him to add: "(here) Frenhofer, (here) Giacometti." In the same spirit, Baudelaire recounts that Balzac was once standing before a beautiful and melancholy winter landscape, portraying a number of huts and wretched peasants. There is "une maison nette" with smoke curling out of it. Beautiful, says Balzac. But what are they thinking? What are they doing? What are their sorrows? Was the harvest good? *Undoubtedly they have bills to pay*. Baudelaire, without irony, suggests this is an excellent lesson in criticism. Appreciate the picture by what it does to you not by what it does on the canvas: "la somme d'idées ou de rêveries qu'il apportera dans mon esprit" not the "formules évocatoires du sorcier".

In sections 2 and 3 of this essay I shall attempt to describe what happens on the surface of Balzac's canvas in the very telling of this highly stylised story, classically restricted in terms of place, time and action, this densely woven web of cross-referential elements, this (meta)-fiction machine so deeply instinct with felt thought as to maximise the generation of visionary and prophetic insight. The first chapter takes place in part of one day in three rooms, the second chapter in part of another day in two rooms, one of them the same as a room from the first chapter. There is a brief coda to round the story off. It is necessary too to look beneath the surface at the layers miming the old man's painting. I hope the new reader will come to agree that this is one of the world's great short stories, written with blazing intelligence and passionate force.

A Reading of Chapter One

Chapter one, like chapter two, begins with a visit, a visitation even. An unnamed young painter visits the house of the famous and influential court painter, Master Porbus. In the first paragraph we find the first of several references throughout the story to poetry. As if participating in a ceremony of hieratic initiation (which indeed is to come) the young man crosses a threshold and climbs the stairs. On these stairs which lead to the studio of Porbus he meets an old man with some traits similar to Balzac's own. The old man – in a figure diametrically opposed to the human status of his own painting later – is explicitly and crucially described as a *painting*, a Rembrandt no less, and there is a sense in which he and his painting are two sides of the same coin or canvas, the two-headed unknown masterpiece, but this is not the best reading of the title, as we shall see. It is of some importance that the youth is portrayed as a lover. The two men enter the studio whose detailed description as an implicit painting serves to emphasise the young painter's situation as a prospective initiate. We observe the canvas (page 11 – the first of a few sign-posts to help the reader) 'so far bearing only three or four white strokes'. Then they see Porbus's famous masterpiece, *Marie égyptienne*.

The old man embarks on the first of his major discourses, having first offered to buy the picture, but Balzac finds an excellent reason to prevent this. The old man's wealth and the theme of money have, however, been introduced. There are references to poetry (page 11) which will be picked up in chapter two. There are references to Prometheus (page 12) and to Proteus (page 13), two of the many mythic predecessors animating the story. The historical and technical discussions of art reflect the debates of Balzac's own day albeit in terms of the High Renaissance but *as such* their function is not primary and the extent to which Balzac was helped or influenced is an academic question – what counts, as the careful reader will notice, is that the old man's telling is integrated into the scriptural dynamics of the story. Only the author could have (re-)*worked* the language. The discussions illuminate the old man's eventual destiny: he makes impossible demands of art and therefore must "fail" (but only in quotation marks) and this is why and how Balzac (or the reader) plucks the twentieth century torch out of the fires of a seventeenth century genius invented to incarnate the author's prophetic instinct in his own day. They tell a process.

Porbus himself is shown to fail as a painter for reasons that are not completely clear – not because Balzac does not have the language (though of course the old man does *not*, given the author's deliberate time-warp) and the specialised knowledge to explain the failings of an imaginary picture, but because failure and doubt and anxiety are built into the structure of the story's prophetic necessity. Here and there the old man contradicts himself, at one point saying Porbus is in two minds, fluctuating between 'drawing and colour' (page 12) and ending his discourse (page 15) with the statement that Porbus's 'colour . . . and line . . . complement each other'. But the contradiction is intentional. In this account of the work of the man whose role and function is to serve as go-between, the old man is setting the scene for the eventual dialectic, confrontation and exchange of the two women who give the chapters their names, despite or even because he goes against the grain of Balzac's own declared views of creativity, even in respect of *this* story. 'Let's stop analysing, you will only despair' (page 13) will be picked up later in this chapter and in chapter two. Language does its work over time while the paintings look on. To some extent the discussion on *trompe l'oeil* (page 14) is shadow boxing. The point is that the scene is also being set for the old man's attitude towards his own picture, while clothing it in an anti-realist, subjective Promethean garb. The essence is the swaying, the doubt. The 'hand' (page 13) will be echoed by the 'foot' in chapter two, while the reference to Raphael (page 14) is interesting, Raphael – the old man's hero – who will be supplanted by the time of the actual writing of the story by Poussin himself as the exemplary man/painter. 'On the surface' (page 14) mirrors and perhaps contradicts the various crucial references to 'underneath' which we will come to.

The unnamed youngster is angered by what he takes to be the old man's wrongheadedness and lack of respect, owns up to being a painter and is invited to attempt a copy. The old man likes it; the reverse won't be true later. Successful, the born painter can be named, in the first of several fulfilled postponements, a key narrative device. He signs himself Nicolas Poussin, no mere novice now but an initiate. He at last "has a name" and can be given a lesson by the master he did not originally come to visit. And the old man sets to (page 15), the old man who is himself a painting, working in a studio which is a painting, on a painting which is a painting (and a woman); the old man goes over – after the young man has copied – the go-between's painting. He is a lover, with a sexual beard and a sexual brush, his task to bring the saint to life, the first reference to another major mythic theme in the story, Pygmalion. During this second discourse and description, Mabuse – the old man's teacher with the auto-sexual name (Poussin *s'abuse* in chapter two: Onan anon as it were) – is brought in (page 16) in such a way as to suggest that Poussin should be the old man's pupil and heir; finally his Catherine Lescault is named, no longer the *Belle Noiseuse* of earlier published texts, but still flowing, a river of a woman (l'Escau) with just a hint of Manon. The old man remains unnamed. Of course *Marie égyptienne* cannot be anywhere as near as beautiful as Catherine though the latter can only be completed and perfected, that is seen (known, fucked, sold) after . . . but this comes later. We note that he, crucially, applies 'layers of colours' (page 16) and also: 'No one will thank us for what is underneath', which will be rhymed elsewhere and in particular during the tragic dénouement.

The story now moves to the old man's house to which, after a laying on of hands and the purchase of Poussin's drawing, the rich old man invites his confrères for a splendid lunch. The contrast between his wealth and Poussin's poverty enters the story in several details. Then at lunch Poussin is agog at a masterpiece on the wall, Mabuse's *Adam*, painted – be it noted – for a good sound financial reason. The picture fails, naturally, just as *Marie égyptienne* does. 'There is nothing but a man there' (page 17) echoes, rhymes, the identical remark(s) about a woman later. Poussin is dumbfounded by another masterpiece he takes to be a Giorgione and further dumbfounded by the old man's dismissal of it as one of his own 'early daubs'. Calling the host 'the God of painting', Poussin finally learns from Porbus that his name is Frenhofer. Porbus now introduces the crucial gynaecomorphic element when he asks to see Frenhofer's 'mistress', which viewing is essential for his growth as an artist. Porbus the go-between turns the story on a pivot.

Frenhofer now embarks on his third major discourse, and confesses his picture is still unfinished, even though she breathes; there

41

is a hint of sexual love. Again, the discourse draws upon technical knowledge Balzac acquired from reading or conversations, but the crucial element is the doubting. As for our leitmotifs: here (page 18) he 'remove[s] layer after layer' (elsewhere he will add layer after layer) from Titian's paintings, and we realise that if he can "undress" a Titian he can "undress" his own painting later just as his eye will, in Balzac's own word, 'undress' Gillette. His remark 'therefore I have not clearly highlighted' (page 19) announces his own picture. He ends the main part of the discourse by echoing Balzac's own stated views about 'too much knowledge' – his doubts, cloning or cloned by Giacometti's (see pages 51–2), set up the later speech by Porbus. But almost at once, in the explicit reference to Pygmalion, he cheers up: all the same, the charge of hubris against Frenhofer must be heavily qualified even if hypothetically we accept the common view that he is a failure.

The matrix of his doubt consists in his understandably not realising that his destiny is to be the incarnation of a prophecy. After the aforementioned reference to Pygmalion – and our story is of course among so many other myths and things a marvellous version of this myth, with hints of the painter Apelle – the speech ends with the old man playing with his knife, perhaps an implied sexual image in the light of Poussin's obvious and virtually explicit sexual dagger in chapter two. Porbus's comment about 'spirit' reads like an unintended joke on Balzac's part with or without sexual connotation and brings to mind Rodin's Balzac. . . . In the following paragraph Poussin's thoughts are reported in free indirect speech by the narrator. The old man is described as something more than a man, a prince, a supernatural being, 'art itself' . . . And then the wonderful flight of the figure of the crazy nature of artists, 'that white-winged girl' (page 20). 'Nature . . . fecund and barren': "Poussin", heeding Porbus *and* Frenhofer who are his parents, will one day be fecund outside the story. Frenhofer continues and concludes his discourse with a crucial hint of the development and outcome of the tragedy, for 'the faultless woman' whom, like Orpheus, he would seek even in hell (page 20) is round the corner in Poussin's lodgings in rue de la Harpe (which is two or three minutes from Frenhofer's house at the Pont Saint-Michel, though the three men's walk there from Porbus's studio would have taken about twenty minutes) literally as it were, awaiting Poussin's return, around the next corner of the narrative. And then Frenhofer makes a pivotal rhyme with his reference to Venus, whose naming in the later description (ah the scriptural!) of Frenhofer's own picture draws together several key strands in the story. We note too that Frenhofer would give up what remains of (see below, Porbus on Mabuse) his entire fortune to become yet another mythic figure (Orpheus, as already mentioned) on the layered surface of the tale, though it is impossible not to be reminded of three other mythic figures who are not mentioned in the story: Faust, Daedalus and Frenhofer's near contemporary, Dr Frankenstein. *Frankenstein* was published in England in 1818 and available in French around 1820, in time for Balzac to read it though I can find no reference to it in his correspondence.

Porbus (pages 20–1) now explains to Poussin about the human founder of the line which via Frenhofer will link Poussin to the Renaissance and ultimately to the first man. This is Mabuse, painter of *Adam*, late teacher of his one and only pupil Frenhofer. This fascinating speech – perhaps the speech of that exalted worker Balzac who actually delivered the goods, wrote masterpieces against the grain of the madness which is part of the Romantic agenda: the Balzac too who famously said "One night of love, one less book" and who, if the Goncourts are to be believed, preferred foreplay to his own orgasm (which doubtless made him a serious and unselfish partner) because ejaculation meant he lost the latest ideas in his head – this fascinating speech reveals the structural aspect of commerce in the narrative: money in exchange for 'the secret ... of endowing his figures with life' which turns out to be, and yet as we know, cannot only be, a ludicrous *trompe l'oeil*. He ends with a clarion call to work, which later Emile Bernard will use word for word in respect of Cézanne.

Poussin returns to his humble lodgings (page 21), to his mistress who is more subtle and less conventional as a person than commonly admitted, though she is more of a *literary* stereotype than all of the other characters. This Gillette is well named, as Audrey Jones has commented, for she ought to have a razor blade concealed about her person, to dispatch her lover who forgets he is living in the wrong century for that kind of behaviour. Whether he is a liar or a self-deceiver is immaterial. Either way everybody knows he will dump Gillette. It should be noted that well before the Frenhofer episode she has already noticed that Poussin's 'eyes no longer speak to me' when she is modelling, which – as Didi-Huberman points out – is why our museums are filled with Poussin's paintings rather than Frenhofer's! Like Frenhofer, Poussin is portrayed as a lover *and* as a painter (the same phrase is used about both of them), and it is now clear their destinies are interlocked. Poussin's attempted reassurance to Gillette that 'Frenhofer will see only the female form in you' echoes Frenhofer's remark about the painting of Adam by Mabuse. Finally we note that fame, wealth and happiness are interlinked: 'I can be a great man! ...

43

We'll be rich, happy. There is gold in these brushes' (page 22).

A Reading of Chapter Two

Three months later Porbus visits Frenhofer to offer a deal, a deal which is the nucleus, the heart of the story, a deal offered by the middle-aged go-between, the middle-man painter of the middle-woman/mediatrix person, *Marie égyptienne*, who is both saint and whore. It effectively involves an exchange of two women, two virgin saints (one in earlier versions an ex-courtesan and one, who knows, a future courtesan or streetwalker) who will become whores "in the eyes" of the other's man. Poussin the painter/lover will allow his model/mistress to be seen (known/fucked/sold) by another man, so that the latter, satisfied that she does not match up to his Catherine, can allow Catherine to be seen (known etc) by Poussin and, secondarily, by Porbus (whose own woman has not been neglected by the two geniuses) so that Porbus can learn from Frenhofer's technique and improve his art, and Poussin – the initiatory secret of art having been confirmed or, if you like, secreted – can become consecrated as a mature genius, a member of the brotherhood of initiated, individuated artists, alone in their studios, which the Romantic movement bequeaths to posterity and of whom this story anachronistically may provide the first example in literature. Modern art begins here.

Frenhofer is tempted by the deal but cannot yet agree. 'Poetry and women reveal themselves naked only to their lovers.' His doubts are at the heart of the story as told and certainly reflect Balzac's ambivalence concerning the relationship of the arts to commerce, always more problematic in painting than in literature. In the end of course Frenhofer does display her but it all goes wrong, as it must. Poussin survives the rainbow of Frenhofer's will, and we ask ourselves if we are confused by our hindsight knowledge of his glorious future. As it is, Frenhofer we are told is too rich to paint, Poussin too poor. The middle-aged and comfortable court painter, absolute bourgeois *avant la lettre*, delivers the goods. If these men are not elements of a composite personality structure they are certainly Pessoan heteronyms.

Frenhofer (page 26) describes himself as 'father, lover, God'. Catherine, in an oft-quoted phrase, is a 'creature not a creation'. And he loves her. How can she be displayed, least of all to another man, especially a younger man, very especially a painter? He hints at the dénouement of the story: 'Yes I shall have the strength to burn . . .' though he cannot know it will be done the next day. The description of Catherine on the couch (page 27) retains the pictural atmosphere of the courtesan she was described as in the earlier versions, though Balzac was surely right to drop all mention of the word courtesan and in this way, by removing an unhelpful ambiguity, emphasize the virgin aspect, making her more completely the counterpart of Gillette in the functional economy of the narrative. It was necessary, but a pity, to lose her nickname, *La Belle Noiseuse*, the argumentative beauty, as it gave an insight into her (and by poetic extension Frenhofer's) character unconnected with her profession. I sometimes wish Catherine had been a painter, a dedicated painter, but this would have been dodgy, too Borgesian perhaps. The old man is absolutely felt and written as a sexual being, a Balzac to his extremities (as is Porbus, though in other, less physical ways). Of the links between art and love and sexuality and death there is no disputing.

Poussin and Gillette arrive. She knows what's what. They meet Porbus (page 27). René Guise finds it surprising that Porbus was 'surpris par la beauté de Gillette', given that he has praised her beauty a few minutes earlier but this is naive on his part since a woman's beauty is always manifold, always various, and I have allowed for this by translating 'caught him by surprise' rather than 'surprised him'. Guise has not noticed (and nor has anyone else) that Porbus must have met Gillette during the three month interval between the two chapters, despite the implication of the first sentence of chapter two that they had not met, else how would Porbus *know* she is so perfect and beautiful? (Unless Balzac has nodded.) In chapter one Gillette appears only in private with Poussin, who at no point even mentions her to his two friends.

Gillette's comment about the immortality of a painter's rejected lover being 'upon your palette' can be read as bitter or bittersweet. I plump for the former. They go in. 'Frenhofer gave a start . . .': in this paragraph (page 27) the lover/artist duality in both men is fused quite magically. Frenhofer agrees to the exchange, as he must, though as the king he has more to lose than has the pretender. For the second time Gillette observes that Poussin is more interested in art than in her, and once again her observation is independent of Frenhofer, for the girl – compared just previously by the narrator to a Georgian girl – catches Poussin deep in contemplation of the picture he had previously taken for a Giorgione. These near homophones, taken in conjunction with the mirror in chapter one and the forthcoming 'petrification' in this chapter, lead to a warranted assumption of the Gorgon as a myth in the kitty of the story. Gillette concedes defeat and goes upstairs, while Poussin makes a terrible threat: he will set the house on fire if the girl cries out. This, as we shall see, is chilling, for the house or rather the pictures will indeed be put to the flame (thus fulfilling both men's prophecy) and Poussin will have been responsible. At the same time, as will also be seen, he is a fibber.

Porbus makes some absurd comments to fill the vacuum, absurd because they are at once obviously true and obviously unnecessary. There is a strong hint of masturbation (remember Mabuse, alors Poussin *s'abuse*) in the gripping of Poussin's dagger (page 29) while he attempts to listen to the fucking (head or body trip it's all the same) and the whole scene is deeply melodramatic – enough ink has been spilled on this latter aspect of Balzac's work – not least in respect of this story and the origins of its first version in Hoffmann and the tradition of the *conte fantastique* (see Laubriet and Castex etc). We note that Frenhofer has now made love to all three women – Gillette here, Catherine as his mistress and *Marie égyptienne* in the reworking of Porbus's painting. Anyway having done whatever he has done with Gillette, Frenhofer (all eye, beard and brush) lets them in. At last it is Poussin's turn to "know" the other woman but you would expect them, wouldn't you, to look first for Gillette, given their concern earlier. Not on her life. They look for the perfected picture (page 29), perfected be it noted, in the only way it can be because it has been compared to (human) imperfection, not because it has been "finished" as such. They look first at another picture, the wrong one says the old man. And they can't find the right one precisely because they are looking for a picture, when they should be looking for a woman. So Frenhofer has to identify his Galatea for them, and in so doing delivers himself (page 29) of a recapitulation of technical aspects, in some ways contradicting earlier statements.

The two men have problems with the canvas, then, suddenly, imperceptibly, magically, Balzac begins the final movement of the drama with Frenhofer's (query) concession that 'it's a canvas all right' and with his 'naive gesture'. His world is about to come apart. Then, Poussin's coup de grâce: 'I see nothing there but confused masses of colours contained by a multitude of strange lines, forming a high wall of paint'. And now, as in some analytical cubist painting, a mimetic element appears to their gaze, a foot, which 'petrifies' them like Lot's wife. The Gorgon-like petrification is appropriate indeed, for the foot is compared in a marvellous figure to Venus (page 30 earlier), this time a Venus *in marble* rising from a city destroyed by fire. This too announces the end of the story. Immediately after the Venus image Porbus says 'There is a woman underneath' (page 30) as if we were dealing with a pentimento rather than a palimpsest. It suggests to me that the woman *could* be made out under the layers (clothes) – he doesn't say "There must be a woman underneath whose foot is all that survives etc, etc". The tragedy is not what the two painters and Balzac and all the early critics think it was, namely that he mistakenly thought he was perfecting his picture year after layer after year after layer, but that he did perfect it during the creative process quote unquote the last two words: and now *instead of looking at the picture properly* they are doing what Frenhofer asked them to do which is look for a woman which is why they couldn't find it in the first place! Not being in the business of prediction, Frenhofer in the seventeenth century (alright, the 19th) cannot know his picture is a perfect artefact of the twentieth century and so he has to die. The other two cannot know this either and they therefore have to remain in ignorance. What on earth or in heaven did they expect in the way of revelation? We have to be grateful that the story itself survives as the foot, like Keats' *Living Hand*, "warm and capable of earnest grasping", published one year after the final version of Balzac's story. Frenhofer, in this reading, with ordinary eyes (or with second sight or in his madness etc) talks about the way he painted part of Catherine's face.

Poussin announces 'there is nothing on his canvas' (page 31). The old man, naturally furious, hurls insults at Poussin sexually and generally, Poussin the young pretender whose victory is problematic, pyrrhic. Perhaps he learns a lesson. And yet what will Nicolas Poussin (often 'le Poussin' in the story) become if not a supreme artist fusing the best of Frenhofer and Porbus (*mutatis mutandis* Balzac himself)? Just as we now have Poussin paintings because he saw Gillette only as a model so we have no Frenhofer picture(s) because he saw Catherine only as a lover (this opposition would be organised differently if the *Belle Noiseuse* had survived into the text I translated from). Well now, Gillette, forgotten, is heard weeping in a corner. She, like the woman underneath, has been busy sending them her regards, and like the woman underneath goes unheeded. Men! But unlike Catherine she is both thin-skinned and out of her depth. It is her end. As for Catherine the proceedings are beneath her. *Habeas corpus.* Frenhofer covers her, his child, his sister, his lover, with a shroud, described in terms of commerce. He too has to die. The tone of his farewell foretells his death. Whether suicide or broken heart is not made clear and is unimportant, it amounts to the same thing.

Textual

The Story

The *Comédie humaine* consists of three main sections, *Etudes analytiques*, the least important, consisting mainly of the *Physiologie du mariage*; *Etudes de moeurs*, sub-divided into six parts and containing the major novels; and the *Etudes philosophiques* whose *romans philosophiques* include Balzac's mystical writings such as *Séraphita*, and books about "the ravages of thought" in which characters self-destruct, eg *Louis Lambert*, *La Peau de chagrin* and *La Recherche de l'absolu*. The second part of this third section is entitled *Contes philosophiques* in which we find a sub-group containing three stories linked by a common theme, one of which is *Le Chef-d'oeuvre inconnu*. The other two stories, *Gambara* and *Massimilla Doni* deal with artistic creation in respect of musical composition and execution respectively. Doctrines such as angelism and those associated with Swedenborg are an important influence in the *Etudes philosophiques*, and therefore the use of the noun 'arcane' is probably anachronistic in our story.

The story first appeared in two issues of the magazine *L'Artiste* in 1831. It was sub-titled "conte fantastique" and the chapters were entitled "Maître Frenhofer" and "Catherine Lescault". Its origins in Hoffmann have been discussed at length in Laubriet's major scholarly work in which the 1831 and 1837 texts are printed side by side. The text in *L'Artiste* was expanded and corrected for the edition of *Romans et contes philosophiques* (volume three) later in 1831. The sub-title was dropped. Chapter one was now entitled "Gillette". New editions containing minor changes appeared after 1831. The story was radically expanded for the edition of *Etudes philosophiques* published in 1837 (the year of the important letter to Hanska) and it is the additions made here which have given rise to the long-running debate (well over a hundred years) about the help Balzac did or did not get from Gautier or Delacroix etc (see pages 55–6 for further discussion and bibliographical leads). 1845 was the year when the volume containing the story in the Furne edition of the *Comédie humaine* was published. The text is virtually identical to 1837. Balzac added the enigmatic dedication in this edition.

The text of the story contained in the edition of Balzac published in 1847, *Le Provincial à Paris*, differs from that of 1845 and does not contain all the corrections Balzac made in his own copy of the latter. Volume ten of the Pléiade edition contains René Guise's text of the story edited for the first time from the 1847 text and from the hand-corrected copy of Furne. According to Guise's article in Heinich our story is one of the rare texts of Balzac with different corrections in both places. In the same article he makes the very important point that the story was re-named "Gillette" in *Le Provincial à Paris* and he suggests possible reasons for this. He goes on to admit that "the weight of Balzacian tradition is such that in the recent . . . Pléiade edition we did not dare adopt this new title". I am under no such burden and therefore mine is the first edition to give the story its final name as intended by Balzac, though whether a final version should always and in every case be privileged is a matter for scholars which I am not inclined to tangle with (see Charles Rosen on this).

After the 1845 publication of *Le Chef-d'oeuvre inconnu* Balzac decided to drop all references to Catherine as a courtesan and all references to her nickname of *La Belle Noiseuse*, the argumentative beauty. An important meditation on "La Belle Noiseuse" is contained in Michel Serres' book *Genèse*. Fertile of insight, it now becomes – especially if the Pléiade text finds itself universally accepted – a case study in the problematics of revised versions. In the article referred to above Charles Rosen has discussed this matter as it affected the Romantic movement including Balzac, and the only Balzac text he refers to in an ostensible discussion of the entire *Comédie humaine* is, yes, *The Unknown Masterpiece*.

The Translation

I translated from the Pléiade text not because it post-dates the 1845 version used by everybody else but because I think the small changes, with one exception, are all improvements. The one exception concerns the last word in chapter one. Balzac dropped the earlier last word: 'qu'auparavant' (now). I have restored it because I think it is needed. You may not agree. Two of the three previous translators (see bibliography for publication details) amusingly misunderstand "Noiseuse" as "Noisette" and Catherine becomes "The Beautiful Hazelnut". But, as a writer and translator, I do not really want to comment on my translation: I "submit me to your judgment/which will be just" in the words of a famous early poem by Menard author F. T. Prince. Translations are always provisional and serious suggestions for improvement (eg the four swearwords) as well as intelligent criticisms will be considered and perhaps acted upon in future editions. The two old versions (1899 and 1908) are mainly of antiquarian interest and belong to the sociology of literature, sub-section late Victorian and Edwardian translations, an extremely interesting topic for somebody else. A recent American translation is incomplete and generally inadequate: it paraphrases, shortens, explains and abridges. So mine is the first new translation in England for eighty years and the first complete translation anywhere for the same period.

The Literature

I will end this section of my essay with some random references to the literature which has grown around our story. Two stories by Henry James rework *Gillette: The Madonna of the Future* which refers to it directly and, to a lesser extent, *The Sweetheart of Monsieur Briseux*. There is a strong hint of the Balzac story in a story by Stefan Zweig (himself a biographer of Balzac) *Die Unsichtbare Sammlung (The Invisible Collection)*. Zola's *L'Oeuvre*, inspired mainly by Cézanne, unquestionably has its roots in Balzac's story though Zola indignantly denied it. We may want to read its influence on or at least kinship with Flaubert's *L'Education sentimentale*, the Goncourt's *Manette Solomon*, as well as the most famous books of Huysmans and Oscar Wilde; and the story is paralleled in Poe's *Oval Portrait*, which was translated by Baudelaire. Gérard Genette makes a persuasive case that several passages in Proust are a kind of literary reply to our story. Then there is Browning's Andrea del Sarto: "I, painting from myself and to myself". The story meant a lot to Baudelaire, the Baudelaire of the poems *Hymne à la beauté* and *La Mort des artistes* which is possibly a direct meditation on *The Unknown Masterpiece*. And Yeats makes a curious connection between Pound's Cantos and the story in the introduction to his notorious Oxford anthology of modern verse. Lastly: Karl Marx. Our story was one of his favourite works. Like Cézanne, his near contemporary, Marx saw himself as Frenhofer, if his son-in-law Lafargue is to be believed – on the grounds that he identified with the Faustian aspect of the painter. Peter Demetz calls this "a friendly, if quite vague conjecture". Demetz's own theory is that Marx sensed (correctly if indeed he did – AR) the intuition of breakdown and revolution in terms of painting in the story, and saw this as homologous to the social revolution. This too is surely "a friendly, if quite vague conjecture". Anyway in a letter of February 25, 1867 Marx recommends the story to Engels as a "chef-d'oeuvre full of delightful irony".

'Yes, yes, it's a canvas all right'

Giacometti

Harold Rosenberg in *Art on the Edge* makes a conventional and boring comment on the story: "the masterpiece turns out to be a mess" etc, and he does something similar in his essay on Giacometti in the same book, but at least he spots the connection. He emphasizes Giacometti's debt to surrealism but quotes enough to show that he understands the central creative tension, the dialectical equilibrium in the work of one of the most prodigiously gifted artists of all time – the *as-if* rejection or actual rejection of aesthetic values, emerging on the other side of *trompe l'oeil* metaphysics like Frenhofer, to approach the absolute, to lie in wait for it, like a character of his friend Beckett. Giacometti designed the tree in *Waiting for Godot* at Beckett's request for Jean-Louis Barrault's production in 1963. The links between Beckett and Giacometti, as Hohl documents, are very serious.

Gaëtan Picon, that incomparable writer on literature and painting, in his centrally important memorial essay on Giacometti, quotes him: "Je recommence tout. Si ça ne va pas mieux dans quinze jours, j'arrête totalement, non? ... Enfin, demain peut-être". The sense of doubt, failure and anxiety built into Frenhofer, central in Cézanne, culminates in some major twentieth century artists: Rothko, Newman, de Kooning and, above all, Giacometti. I refer the reader to Hohl's monograph on Giacometti in which there are many implicit and explicit references to *The Unknown Masterpiece*. A major turning point for the artist was his portrait of Yanaihara, involving a crisis of representation and one documented by Giacometti statements from which Hohl quotes: "Since then [1956] things have been going from bad to worse", but the solution to the crisis had the impossibility of "realisation" built into it. "Giving up painting and sculpture seemed to me such a very sad idea that I didn't even feel like getting up in the morning and eating. So I started to work again"; then a comment to Yanaihara which is pure Frenhofer: "I don't know if it's good or bad, but I don't really care. I'm going on no matter what ... *Never in my life have the possibilities been so good*. ... Five minutes ago your face was as good as finished. ... Even your eyes were exactly right. But it's all gone again. There's nothing left to see on the canvas". James Lord's *Portrait of Giacometti* is full of such remarks. And then a few weeks before he died: "I've made tremendous progress: now I can make advances in my work only by turning back on its goal; now I create only by destroying". Hohl even argues that

51

Giacometti's paintings of this period could be used to illustrate the story.

In the story itself there are various bits that Giacometti could have written for Balzac (just as people have argued that Gautier or Delacroix or A. N. Other wrote parts of it) for example the passage on sculpture in Frenhofer's first major discourse (page 13). The later passage beginning 'Show you my work' (page 18) containing the section 'we draw by modelling ... background and contours meet' shows what one is tempted to call a premonition on Balzac's part of Giacometti's drawings and paintings of the 1950s. I do not want to leave the impression that only Giacometti and a few other artists have experienced the sense of failure, doubt and anxiety we have been discussing – what is at stake is its structure as a central creative principle.

Cézanne

It is well known that Cézanne was obsessed by Balzac's story. Gasquet: "Il s'enfonça dans la recherche de l'absolu [possibly a direct reference to a related novel by Balzac – AR]. Il fut seul. Il travailla. Le volume des *études philosophiques* [containing *The Unknown Masterpiece* – AR] tout fripé, sâli et décousu, était un de ses livres de chevet." And Bernard: "Un soir que je lui parlais du *Chef-d'oeuvre inconnu* et de Frenhofer ... il se leva de table, se dressa devant moi, et frappant sa poitrine avec son index, il s'accusa, sans un mot, mais par sa geste multiplié, le personnage même du roman. Il en était si ému que des larmes emplissaient ses yeux." It is not because the story anticipates his theories and practice, though it does, that Cézanne identified with Frenhofer, but because he rightly sensed the influence of anxiety, the psychic prefiguration of himself. Rilke tells the story of Cézanne and Frenhofer in his important letter to Clara of October 9, 1907. He describes Cézanne's "problem of realisation" and talks of Balzac's "unbelievable vision of future evolutions".

Kurt Badt in the important chapter on "realisation" in his book on Cézanne argues that Balzac had an intimate knowledge of the problems facing Romantic painters. He explains how doubt and anxiety were in the air – eg Delacroix, Daumier, Frenhofer, and that Cézanne (and Zola) both felt that the impressionists *did* not deliver, and that he, Cézanne, *could* not deliver. Badt argues that the key writer is Castagnary with his concept of realisation – essentially the problem of subjectivity which was ignored by academics, and that Frenhofer is the first artist to undergo the terrible experience of subjectivity and could not survive the failure of realisation. This must await the later developments intuited and foreshadowed by Balzac.

Washington Allston

Nathaniel Hawthorn's wonderful story, *The Artist of the Beautiful*, brings Balzac to mind. I am having an affectionate dispute about influence with my old friend and Menard author, Paul Auster, who – if you have read his *New York Trilogy* – is an expert influence-monger and may or may not be teasing me. He is sure that Balzac had heard of the painter Washington Allston who is mentioned in Hawthorn's story and undoubtedly inspired it. He thinks Allston could be the model for Frenhofer. The dates fit but so far I am unimpressed by the argument, which is mere conjecture. Perhaps, indeed, Hawthorn read the Balzac story?

Allston was the contemporary of David and Turner (reads like Gilbert and George) and the first major Romantic painter of America. As early as 1805 he gave America a colouristic style. He also coined the term "objective correlative" as long ago as the 1830s, a term Eliot does not admit stealing. Allston travelled in Europe and made a famous portrait of his friend, Coleridge. But the important point about him is that he spent twenty-five years on the same painting, his *Belshazzar's Feast*, begun in 1817; he worked on it until the day of his death and left it unfinished. It hangs in Detroit. He was able to work on it because some New England ladies organised a grant for him of ten thousand dollars to free him of financial burdens (cf Frenhofer) but as R. Dana said: 'That is his shroud." One comment from Allston: "I have today blotted out four years work on my 'handwriting on the wall'."

Picasso

In *Life with Picasso*, a source to be treated with circumspection, Françoise Gilot quotes her future partner as saying "that covered spiral staircase you walked up to get here is the one the young painter in Balzac's *Le Chef-d'oeuvre inconnu* climbed when he came to see old Porbus, Poussin's friend, who painted pictures nobody understood", and the book contains a photo of Picasso on the staircase. And indeed in the upper room of the house on rue des Grands-Augustins, formerly Jean-Louis Barrault's studio as well as Porbus's, Picasso painted *Guernica!* But equally interesting are the lapses in Picasso's comment – if reported accurately by Gilot. They provide circumstantial evidence that Picasso may not have read the text all that carefully before preparing his *livre d'artiste* edition for Vollard. Certainly it was fascinating to learn and observe (in the company of the painter Julia Farrer in the Victoria and Albert Museum) how the illustrations to the text itself (haphazardly arranged) differ from the work preceding the rather bad essay by Albert Besnard whose contribution no one has satisfactorily explained.

It is in 1927, the year he met Marie-Thérèse Walter, that the painter/model theme appears for the first time in Picasso, in drawings and etchings some of which were made for the 1931 Vollard edition, some of which were done independently before he received the commission, and both groups contain his most abstract work to that date. The reader is referred to Heinich's book for a major essay by Thierry Chabanne on Picasso and Balzac. The Vollard book is an important element in the iconography of our story. Giacometti visited the studio at rue des Grands-Augustins. He must at some point have read the story but there is no mention of this in Lord or Hohl. In any case, the story reads him.

Van Gogh and others

In July 1883 Van Gogh wrote: "Zola has this in common with Balzac, that he knows little about painting . . . Balzac's painters are enormously tedious, very boring". Whether or not this is true about the novelist's other painters it is surely quite wrong about Frenhofer, which leads me to conclude that despite the fact that Van Gogh read widely and deeply in Balzac he somehow missed *The Unknown Masterpiece*. My suspicion is reinforced by a remarkable letter of August 1888 in which Van Gogh writes: "Degas lives like a humble lawyer and does not like women, for he knows that if he loved them and fucked them often he, intellectually diseased, would become insipid as a painter. . . . Ah Balzac, that great and powerful artist, has rightly told us that relative chastity fortifies the modern artist." Now Degas is no Frenhofer but we are in adjacent territory and Van Gogh, had he read the story, surely "might have passed some remark", to quote a character of Beckett, about this.

In his conversations with Matisse, the poet Francis Carco reports that the painter in 1941 was having problems and had spent three months on one still life. Carco wanted to tell him about our story, ie too much revision blah blah. There is another anecdote: concerning Matisse's famous 1914 portrait of Yvonne Landsberg: her mother did not like it and it reminded her of Balzac's "[incomprehensible] masterpiece". According to Barr its lines are unprecedented and anomalous in Matisse and influenced by the futurists. It was re-covered at each sitting.

Mark Rothko wrote in 1958: "It was with the utmost reluctance that I found the figure could not serve my purposes ... But a time came when none of us could use the figure without mutilating it." Harold Rosenberg writes in *The Anxious Object* that for de Kooning "painting 'The Woman' was a mistake. It could not be done. Esthetically, the canvas is an inadequate expression of the artist's experience and intention ... For authority for such a creation, which defies the medium, de Kooning could turn to Balzac's *The Unknown Masterpiece* which then occupied his thought." De Kooning also said that Frenhofer's painting predicted cubism. Lukacs told Alfred Wurmser that in his opinion Balzac posed the problem of neo-impressionism in this story.

Art History

For well over a hundred years art historians and literary scholars have disputed the influences on the "theoretical" passages in the story, especially Frenhofer's three discourses, but I think these readers magnify out of all recognition what is really a minor problem – did he write the passages himself/he couldn't have/who helped him/wrote them for him etc, etc – because they abstract their own concerns from his: they are more interested in art history than in literature. It must be stated plainly that this is a story, a story in which a great writer's words are doing their own kind of work or being made to do their own kind of work: the passages in question interlink and connect with passages that are not in question. The disputed passages contain contradictions and naïvetes, but nothing is there which does not cunningly contribute to the economy, logic and beauty of the story. That said, I shall try to point the reader in the direction of the arguments.

We know that Balzac read Diderot. He knew personally Gautier and Delacroix and dedicated *La Fille aux yeux d'or* to the latter in 1834 (it has also been suggested that the Lord of the dedication to our own story is the anglophile Delacroix). Undoubtedly there are striking similarities to Delacroix's *Journals* on for example the subject of line and contour, but the *Journals* were not published until years later; Fosca, however, asserts that Balzac "pumped" Delacroix as was his wont with specialists of all kinds; Gilman thinks that this is possible. Eigeldinger, in the notes to his edition, argues strongly in favour of the influence of Delacroix on the problems of pictorial technique and creation while Guise and Gilman, more plausibly in my opinion, settle for Diderot, who also influenced Balzac in other areas. Diderot's ideas on vision, expression and technique are close to Balzac's but as Gilman rightly points out the novelist reworked them, as he would be bound to. Guise nods also in Gautier's direction and, dismissing the "pumping" idea, suggests Balzac and Delacroix were both reacting to common stimuli. M. Wingfield Scott dismisses the Gautier hypothesis (popular in the nineteenth century) and is not convinced that Delacroix's ideas were that close to Balzac's, though she thinks it possible he may have chipped in. But she rightly insists and indeed demonstrates that it was all reworked and not just inserted, and whoever reworked it wrote the story.

Jerrold Lanes rubbishes Balzac's understanding and knowledge of art and is adamant that Balzac could not have produced such technically advanced ideas on his own, nor coped with the available written sources. He says that "Balzac's tastes . . . are hard to reconcile with Frenhofer's views." This is irrelevant of course. Helen Borowitz draws attention to the possible influence of Victor Cousin and Henri Latouche. Nathalie Heinich, in her own essay in the book she edited, and Dore Ashton both point out that Balzac learned a lot from Boulanger while his portrait was being painted (what one would give for a record of their conversation à la Lord/Giacometti). Heinich also draws attention to the anachronisms in the story: the pantheon of names, the painter born rich/ marginalised loonie, Poussin's ethical irresponsibility, the theme of initiation, the private studios and so on.

What we really want to know is: who prepared the lunch chez Frenhofer for the three painters? Perhaps the old woman sweeping out the room at Porbus's house had two jobs? Perhaps she had been a painter's mistress, fallen on hard times, become a whore, and then returned to the world of art, which as we know, doubles life?

Conclusion

What remains is the story. Like Keats' *Living Hand*, like Giacometti's painted figure described by Sartre as "hallucinatory because it takes the form of an interrogative apparition", like Gillette and Catherine, *Le Chef-d'oeuvre inconnu* – a parable of writing the more powerful for not being about writers – sends us its regards. Quite apart from the fact that painting was considered superior to literature as description, it made good sense for Balzac in this parable to metamorphose a (the) writer's agony and ecstasy into that of a painter for otherwise he would have had to *write* what he is not obliged to paint – it is impossible enough to describe a painting (imaginary or real) in words. The parable of writing the writing or painting the painting, the artist's copy letter, is another story, and must await the twentieth century, Pierre Menard for example. Meanwhile, *The Unknown Masterpiece* is a supreme metafiction, a pictural writing telling scriptural paintings. I would not go along with whoever suggested the story was Balzac's sweet revenge on painting. What I say is that the unknown masterpiece is not *merely* Catherine, not even Catherine/Frenhofer (though it *is* of course). After all the necessary discussion and clarification concerning Frenhofer as a successful great painter, as foreshadowing Giacometti, we conclude that the unknown masterpiece *is the story itself*. Balzac knew, and was telling us that it was his finest work. And he knew what he was doing when he changed the title to *Gillette*. For, when all is said and done, a metafiction is also a fiction, in this case a story about love which has the power to astonish us today with its relevance to the post-feminist problem of freedom. Poussin, like Rilke himself, finds it easy to let go. Frenhofer, like those whom Rilke addresses, finds it difficult.

> *So the fault is this, if there is any fault:*
> *not to increase the freedom of a loved one*
> *with all the freedom you find within yourself.*
> *For when we love we have nothing but this:*
> *to let each other go, since holding on*
> *comes easy and we do not have to learn it.*

And now the time has come to draw a (green serge) veil over this essay, this impatient and somewhat edgy essay perhaps typical of a translator breaking free of the constraints imposed by his professional discipline. Time to visit the National Gallery, Room 32, and pause in silence and wonder before Poussin's *Landscape with a Man killed by a Snake*. And Frenhofer? He was one who, as Gertrude Stein said of Picasso, "walked in the light and a little ahead of himself, like Raphael".

Dramatis Personae

Maître Frenhofer

Given the dates of the real painters Mabuse, Poussin and Porbus, Balzac's imaginary painter would have been born around 1540. Since he dies in 1613 he is the exact contemporary of El Greco. There are various theories about his name: see Guise's edition and Wayne Conner's article. Hohl in his monograph on Giacometti dogmatically associates the name with "frénésie". It is undoubtedly not an accident that the name is Germanic, given the limited possibilities open even to Balzac after inventing a character so interested in theory. [*Added at proof stage*. Re-reading *Le Cousin Pons* (1848) recently, I was struck by a passage where Balzac['s narrator] (see below) is rude about Hoffmann (see page 48) and refers pejoratively to the *mens teutonica*. I do not think I want to pursue this too deeply.]

Mabuse

His real name was Jean Gassaert dit de Mabuse, a Flemish painter. According to Eigeldinger he was born in 1470 and died in 1532 while according to Guise he was born in 1499 and died in 1562. Usually the differences of opinion between these two editors are helpful and interesting! In this instance the confusion partly arises because Guise has given as the date of death the date in a book known to have been used by Balzac for documentation, a date which fits the story, or Frenhofer would have had to be much too old. Raitt agrees with Eigeldinger but I shall follow my Quillet-Flammarion encyclopaedia and give 1478–1535, which Gombrich in *The Story of Art* settles for while querying both. Mabuse travelled to England. There is an *Adam* in Hampton Court. And he also visited Italy. According to Guise he was imprisoned for drunkenness rather than for his debts.

Marie the Egyptian

Marie was a whore who renounced the game to retire naked to the desert after a vision and a conversion. Without the money to go over the water to the Holy Land from Egypt she was prepared to "give" herself one more time, to a boatman, as the fare. Marina Warner gives another version in which she works as a whore on the boat and repents at the door of the Holy Sepulchre, but feels her past way of life means she must not go in. Guise dismisses Laubriet's view that an actual portrait of Marie – not by Porbus – inspired the story of Gillette, but his own theory, that Marie is one more example of the thesis of the *Etudes philosophiques* that too powerful an input of ideas and passions is destructive, is equally unlikely. The economical logic of the narrative leads to the simple view that having constructed his Catherine/Gillette opposition, Balzac needed a go-between (just as Porbus "goes between" Frenhofer and Poussin) and inspirationally chose Marie, in a version where she is about to pay and, as Poussin points out, the boatman hesitates.

Porbus

Franz Porbus the Younger was born in Antwerp in 1570. He became a court painter in France after a stay in Rome. He died in 1622. By 1612, the year of the beginning of the story, he was famous and Poussin might well have wanted to meet him. He painted a portrait of Henri IV (as the text says) which is now in the Louvre and of Catherine de Medici. But he never painted a *Marie égyptienne*, as far as is known. For details of the link between his studio and Picasso see elsewhere in this book (pages 53–4).

Poussin

1594–1665. The dates fit the history well. Balzac describes him as 'le Poussin' several times in the story and whether or not – I think he is – he is playing on the name's meaning (the spring chicken), the honorific article is clearly a prefiguration of Poussin's future importance, as in Tasso/le Tasse or Tintoretto/le Tintoret (born the year Poussin died, as it happens). Richard Verdi has written a fascinating article about the iconography of Poussin's life and work as interpreted in the nineteenth century.

Other Characters

Catherine Lescault: the mistress/painting of Frenhofer (see page 49 for details of the *Belle Noiseuse*)

Gillette: the mistress/model of Poussin

An old woman: sweeping out a room (rowing over the water?)

Father Hardouin: who does not make an appearance

Various paintings including Mabuse's *Adam*

A narrator [*Added at proof stage*. The narrator's role deserved proper discussion. It is interesting to note, for example, that Rembrandt – see page 10 – was six years old at the time of the story]

BIBLIOGRAPHY

(Note: place of publication is Paris for French-language books and London for English-language books unless otherwise stated)

1. Balzac texts

La Comédie humaine. Vol. 10. Text presented, established and annotated by René Guise. Gallimard (Bibliothèque de la Pléïade), 1979.

Le Chef-d'oeuvre inconnu (with *Gambara* and *Massimilla Doni*). Edited and introduced by Marc Eigeldinger and Max Milner. Garnier-Flammarion, 1981.

Le Chef-d'oeuvre inconnu. Eaux-fortes originales et dessins gravés sur bois de Pablo Picasso. Vollard, 1931.

Le Chef-d'oeuvre inconnu. Illustrations by Pablo Picasso. Geneva, Skira, 1945.

Short Stories. Edited by A. W. Raitt. Oxford University Press, 1964 (often reprinted).

Note to English readers: this is a useful, accessible and cheap edition of some of Balzac's best stories in the original French, with introduction and notes in English. But NB: the text of the story is that of 1845 (as in Eigeldinger and Milner above) NOT that edited by Guise (above) from the 1847 and Balzac's hand-corrected 1845 texts (used for this translation). See pages 48–9 of my introduction. The bibliography is out of date and the intelligent remarks about our story do not reflect the serious work done in the last twenty years. Time for a second edition, rather than another reprint.

Correspondance. 5 vols. Edited by Roger Pierrot. Garnier, 1960–9.

Lettres à Madame Hanska. 4 vols. Edited by Roger Pierrot. Édit. du Delta, 1967–71.

2. Previous translations

The Unknown Masterpiece in *The Unknown Masterpiece and Other Stories*. Translated by George Burnham Ives. Caxton, 1899.

The Unknown Masterpiece in *Christ in Flanders and Other Stories*. Translated by Mrs Ellen Marriage. Everyman (J. M. Dent), 1908.

The Unknown Masterpiece (incomplete). Translated by Michael Neff. Berkeley (Cal.), Creative Arts, 1984.

3. Books and articles on the story itself

Books

ASHTON, Dore, *A Fable of Modern Art*. Thames and Hudson, 1980.
A fascinating but scrappy and wayward book.

DIDI-HUBERMAN, Georges, *La Peinture incarnée*. Édit. de Minuit, 1985.
A brilliantly inventive, fertile and difficult book which deserves to be translated, but pity the poor translator.

HEINICH, Nathalie, *ed.*, *Autour du Chef-d'oeuvre inconnu*. ENSAD, 1985.
A very important and coherent collection, containing major essays by the editor herself and others including Chabanne, Marin and Lebensztejn. Many illustrations and a comprehensive bibliography which sent me to a number of essential texts.

LAUBRIET, Pierre, *Un Catéchisme esthétique*. Didier, 1961.
Detailed scholarly study of several aspects of the story. It includes the versions of 1831 and 1837.

Articles

BERNARD, Claude E., 'La Problématique de l'échange dans *Le Chef-d'oeuvre inconnu* de Honoré de Balzac', *L'Année balzacienne* no. 4 (1983), pp. 201–213.

BOROWITZ, Helen O., 'Balzac's unknown masters', *Romanic Review* [Syracuse, (N.Y.)], vol. 72 (1983), pp. 425–41.

CONNER, Wayne, 'Balzac's Frenhofer', *Modern Language Notes* [Baltimore, (Md.)], May 1954, pp. 335–8.

EVANS, A. R. *Jr.*, 'The *Chef-d'oeuvre inconnu*: Balzac's myth of Pygmalion and modern painting', *Romanic Review*, vol. 53, no. 3 (1962), pp. 187–98.

EVANS, A. R. *Jr.*, 'Balzac and M. Frenhofer: an iconographic note', *Romance Notes* [Chapel Hill (N.C.)], vol. 5 (1963), pp. 32–7.

FILOCHE, Jean-Luc, '*Le Chef-d'oeuvre inconnu*: peinture et connaissance', *L'Année balzacienne*, no. 1 (1980), pp. 47–59.

GILMAN, Margaret, 'Balzac and Diderot: *Le Chef-d'oeuvre inconnu*', *PMLA* [New York] vol. LXV (1950), pp. 644–8.

HUBERT, R. R., 'The Encounter of Balzac and Picasso', *Dalhousie French Studies* [Dalhousie] V, Oct. 1983, pp. 38–54.

LANES, Jerrold, 'Art criticism and the authorship of the *Chef-d'oeuvre inconnu*: a preliminary study', pp. 86–99 in *The Artist and Writer in France. Essays in honour of Jean Seznec*. Ed. Haskell, Levi and Shackleton. Oxford, Clarendon Press, 1974.

MASSOL-BEDOIN, Chantal, 'L'Artiste ou l'imposture: le secret du *Chef-d'oeuvre inconnu* de Balzac', *Romantisme*, no. 54 (1986), pp. 44–57.
This is a major contribution to the literature on Balzac's story, standing alongside Didi-Huberman's book, Damisch and several of the essays in Heinich.

SHILLONY, Héléna, 'En marge du *Chef-d'oeuvre inconnu*: Frenhofer, Apelle and David', *L'Année balzacienne*, no. 3 (1982), pp. 288–90.

WENT-DAOUST, Yvette, '*Le Chef-d'oeuvre inconnu* de Balzac ou l'écriture picturale', *CRIN* [Groningen], no. 17 (1987), pp. 48–64.

4. Books and articles containing important discussions of aspects of the story

Books

BEGUIN, Albert, *Balzac lu et relu*. Édit. du Seuil, 1965, pp. 229–33.

BONARD, Olivier, *La Peinture dans la création balzacienne*. Geneva, Droz, 1969, esp. pp. 78–90.

CASTEX, P.-G., *Nouvelles et contes de Balzac 11*. CDU, 1961, pp. 36–62.

DAMISCH, Hubert, *Fenêtre jaune cadmium ou les dessous de la peinture*. Edit. du Seuil, 1984, esp. pp. 11–46.

> The above pages have been translated as "The underneaths of painting" by Francette Pacteau and Stephen Bann in the issue of *Word and Image* called *Painting and Sign*, vol. 1, no. 2 (1985), pp. 197–209.

EIGELDINGER, Marc, *La Philosophie de l'art chez Balzac*. Geneva, Cailler, 1957, pp. 58–78.

FOSCA, François, *De Diderot à Valéry; les écrivains et les arts visuels*. Albin-Michel, 1960, pp. 47–67.

GENETTE, Gérard, *Figures 1*. Édit. du Seuil, 1966, pp. 52–5.

JUNOD, Philippe, *Transparence et opacité. Essai sur les fondements théoriques de l'art moderne*. Lausanne, L'Age d'homme, 1976, esp. pp. 70–1, 112–3, 132–3, 258–9.

LEIRIS, Michel, *Au Verso des images*. Montpellier, Fata Morgana, 1986, pp. 45–81.

RICHARD, Jean-Pierre, *Études sur le romantisme*. Édit. du Seuil, 1971, pp. 76–9.

SERRES, Michel, *Genèse*. Grasset, 1982, pp. 27–52.

VANNIER, Bernard, *L'Inscription du corps. Pour une sémiotique du portrait balzacien*. Klincksieck, 1972, pp. 68–72.

WINGFIELD SCOTT, Mary, *Arts and Artists in Balzac's 'Comédie humaine'*. Chicago, 1937, pp. 241–268.

> Note: This thesis is available only on microfilm.

Article

ROSEN, Charles, "Romantic originals", *The New York Review of Books*, vol. XXXIV, no. 20 (Dec. 17th 1987), pp. 22–32.

5. Books and Articles etc. containing brief discussions of the story/background material on Balzac/other related material

Books

ARNHEIM, R., *New Essays on the Psychology of Art*. Berkeley, University of California Press, 1986.

BADT, Kurt, *The Art of Cézanne*. Faber and Faber, 1965.

BARR, A. H., *Matisse, His Art and His Public*. Secker and Warburg, 1975.

BARTHES, Roland, *S/Z*. Edit. du Seuil, 1970.
  Had he lived he would surely have pointed the lucid camera of his gaze at *Gillette*.

BAUDELAIRE, Charles, *Oeuvres complètes*. Gallimard (Pléïade edn.), 1954.

BERNARD, Emile, *Souvenirs sur Paul Cézanne*. H. Laurens, 1924.

CASTEX, P-G., *Le Conte fantastique en France*. Corti, 1951.

CHARLTON, D. G., GAUDON, J., PUGH, A. R., eds., *Balzac and the Nineteenth Century (H. J. Hunt Festschrift)*. Leicester, Leicester University Press, 1972.

CURTIUS, E. R., *Balzac*. Grasset, 1933.

DEMETZ, P., *Marx, Engels and the Poets. Origins of Marxist Literary Criticism*. Chicago, Chicago University Press, 1959.

GASQUET, Joachim, *Cézanne*. Bernheim-Jeune, 1926.

GILOT, Françoise, *Life with Picasso*. New York, Signet, 1965.

HOHL, Reinhold, *A. Giacometti*. Thames and Hudson, 1971.

JAMES, Henry, *Collected Tales*. vol. 3. Hart-Davis, 1962.

KANES, Martin, *Balzac's Comedy of Words*. Princeton, N.J., Princeton University Press, 1975.

KERMODE, Frank, *Romantic Image*. Routledge and Kegan Paul, 1986.

LAUBRIET, Pierre, *L'Intelligence de l'art chez Balzac*. Didier, 1961.

LORD, James, *Giacometti*. Faber and Faber, 1986.

LORD, James, *Portrait of Giacometti*. Faber and Faber, 1981.

MATISSE, Henri, *Matisse on Painting*. Phaidon, 1984.
  Note: contains his conversation with Carco.

MERLEAU-PONTY, Maurice, *Signes*. Gallimard, 1960.

MOSS, A., *Baudelaire and Delacroix*. Nizet, 1973.

PICON, Gaëtan, *Balzac par lui-même*. Edit. du Seuil, 1960.

PORZIO, D., *and* VALSECCHI, M., eds., *Picasso, His Life and Art*. Secker and Warburg, 1979.

PRENDERGAST, C., *Balzac: Fiction and Melodrama*. Arnold, 1978.

RICHARDSON, E. P., *Washington Allston, a Study of the Romantic Artist in America*. Chicago, Chicago University Press, 1948.

RILKE, R. M., *Lettres 1900–1911*. Stock, 1934.

ROSENBERG, Harold, *Art on the Edge*. Chicago, Chicago University Press, 1975.

ROSENBERG, Harold, *The Anxious Object*. Chicago, Chicago University Press, 1982.

SARTRE, Jean-Paul, *Situations V*. Gallimard, 1964.

VAN GOGH, Vincent, *Collected Letters* (3 vols). Thames and Hudson, 1958.

WARNER, Marina, *Monuments and Maidens*. Picador, 1985.

WURMSER, A., *La Comédie inhumaine*. Gallimard, 1964.

YEATS, W. B., ed., *The Oxford Book of Modern Verse*. Oxford University Press, 1936.

ZWEIG, Stefan, *Kaleidoscope*. Cassell, 1934.

Articles, etc.

JONES, Audrey, 'Aspects of fifteenth-century Venetian drawing.' Unpublished thesis. 1971.

JONES, Audrey, 'Neo-Platonism and Renaissance dinner parties.' Unpublished note on *Gillette*. 1988.

PICON, Gaëtan, 'Notes écrites après la mort de Giacometti', *L'Ephémère*, no. 1 (1965).

ROTHKO, Mark, quoted in *Tate Gallery catalogue* (for his exhibition), 1987.

RUSSO, Adelaide, 'Olympia's ribbon: talisman, reliques and other fetishes', *L'Esprit Créateur* [Baton Rouge], vol. XXII, no. 4 (1983), pp. 3–14.

VERDI, Richard, 'Poussin's life in nineteenth-century pictures', *The Burlington Magazine*, Dec. 1969, pp. 741–50.